ARMED WITH
POWER

SHIMMERTREE CHRONICLES BOOK 1

ROBYN OAKES

Armed With Power
Shimmertree Chronicles Book 1

Copyright © 2014 by Robyn Oakes

This is a work of fiction. All characters, organizations, and events portrayed in this novel are either products of the author's imagination or used fictitiously.

Published by
Bird Tree Publishing
Riverton, Utah
www.birdtreepublishing.com

For more creative works by this author visit
www.shimmertree.com

13 ISBN 978-1-941128-01-5
10 ISBN 1941128017

Cover Design: Robert A Jones
Back Cover Illustration: Nele Diel

This book is set in 14 pt Garamond

1

Haefen sat on the sand, mesmerized by the ebb and flow of the waves, his blue eyes mirroring the restless water. The breeze brought the stink of fish from the boats further up the shore, and Haefen's stomach roiled.

The beach grass rustled behind him, and Daniel stepped onto the sand. "I thought I'd find you here. Mama says dinner's ready."

"All right." Haefen stood and brushed the sand off the back of his pants.

"Are you nervous?" Daniel asked, as they threaded their way back through the grass.

"A bit."

Daniel took his hand. "I wish it was me."

Haefen chuckled. "A few more years and it will be. Then you'll be the one staring at the sea, searching for courage in the salty air."

The family had begun to gather around the table when Haefen and Daniel stepped through the doorway.

Their mother smiled. "You found him." She took the pot from the stove and carried it to the table.

Their father chuckled. "The boy couldn't be late for his own birthday meal, could he? Not when you've made all his favorite food."

Haefen slid onto the bench between his little sisters and Daniel. "Thank you, Mama. It smells delicious."

While they ate, Haefen glanced around the table and

tried to memorize all their features. Kerstin and Maerta smiled as they talked about which stories they wanted to tell tonight. Daniel's expression was blissful when he bit into a roll slathered with jam. His parents' eyes filled with love when they met his gaze. It would be three long weeks before he sat here again for an evening meal, when he returned from his journey to Mount Nevo.

When they'd eaten and cleared the table, Haefen's family strolled through the dusk to gather with the rest of the village around the central fire pit. Everyone in Phonteh would celebrate the end of Haefen's childhood and wish him well on his journey.

The rest of the evening passed in a happy blur of stories about Haefen, interwoven with songs he'd loved all his life. Everyone took a turn reminiscing. Last of all, his father told of Haefen arriving in the village, an orphaned babe, and Rohbert and Rute welcoming him into their home. It was a story Haefen had heard many times, but he never tired of it.

Rohbert stood by the dying fire and told the circle of villagers about his broken heart when the sickness took their two sons, and his wife's empty arms that ached for the babes she'd lost. He described the frantic traveler carrying the whimpering baby he'd found, hoping someone in the village would be willing to feed and care for it.

At the end of the story Rohbert turned to Haefen, seated in the place of honor. "My son, you've brought joy to our household, from that first day until now. You healed your mother's heart, and mine. We'll miss you while you're away, but we will rejoice to welcome a man of power back to our hearth."

The evening was over. The men doused the fire, and everyone gathered around to wish Haefen well.

Walking home afterward, Rohbert put his arm around Haefen's shoulders. "There is something I must speak to you about before you sleep." He paused outside their door. "Sit here on the bench with me awhile."

Daniel and the girls trooped inside the house, and Rute smiled at Haefen before she followed them in and shut the door behind her.

Haefen sat on the sturdy wooden bench beside his father. Rohbert must want to give him a few last words of advice and encouragement. They'd often rested there in the evenings, talking about the farm and planning the next day's work.

The stars blazed with an extra brilliance in the dark of the moon. Rohbert gazed at them a moment before turning to face Haefen. "There is something I must caution you about the Qodesh on the mountain. You know you must state your name and your father's name before you'll be allowed to enter. Although your mother and I feel you are truly our son, my name might not suffice. It's never happened before that a son from our village doesn't know the names of his parents. I hope and pray that Abba El deems it acceptable." He gave the heavens a quick glance. "But you must ask the brothers on Mount Nevo before you make your attempt on the Qodesh."

Haefen sat stunned and chilled by his father's words. "Not suffice? Why tell me now? Why not four years ago when I began my studies?"

Rohbert snorted. "So that you could worry all this time?" He pulled a square of paper from his shirt pocket and unfolded it carefully, almost reverently. "The traveler who brought you to us all those years ago gave me this, and told me to give it to you on your sixteenth birthday. Your mother and I have puzzled over it many times. It may lead you to your birth father if you can't enter the Qodesh without his name."

Haefen took the paper and peered at it in the starlight. He made out three brief lines written boldly in black ink:

Begin your search with
the circle in a circle.
"Seek earnestly and ye shall find me."

Haefen recognized the last line from The Book of the Faithful. "Did the traveler say more about this?"

"He told us only what you've heard before, that he found you crying at the campsite with your parents both dead. We've always thought they died of the same sickness that took our sons. I asked the traveler if he had found this paper with your parents, but he only repeated that I should give it to you on your sixteenth birthday. We never even learned his name, and we wouldn't know yours if it hadn't been stitched on your blanket."

"Yes." Haefen had often held the small blanket and stroked the carefully stitched letters, wondering if it were even his name. The blanket might have belonged to another child first, and then been passed down for him to use. The only sure anchor in Haefen's life had been the love of his foster parents, and now that might not be enough.

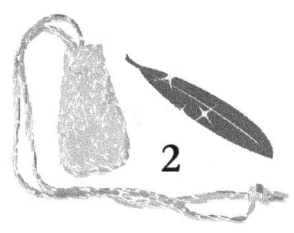

2

"Pleasant Knoll is a pleasant place to live."

Laurelin told herself this over and over, but it didn't convince her that moving to a hick town halfway across the country had been a good thing. She had left behind all her friends and everything she cared about, right before her junior year of high school. Her counselor didn't even know if all her classes would transfer. Apparently Missouri thought Oceanography was a trendy California fad, and not a science.

But the worst thing about moving was leaving her mom behind, or at least where her mother lay buried. Laurelin still couldn't believe her dad had done that. Her jaw tightened just thinking about it.

She wrinkled her nose and shifted in her seat on the bus. The boy beside her smelled a bit ripe, but the breeze from the open window didn't smell any better. One of the cows grazing near the highway lifted its head and watched the bus crawl past. Laurelin grimaced and shifted again. So pleasant to be stuck to a vinyl seat by her own sweat.

The bus was full of kids from the local church youth group headed to a state park for a summer picnic. Back home her friends were probably packed in air-conditioned cars headed for the beach. Laurelin wished she knew how to teleport, or at least had her phone so she could listen to music. But no, her dad had taken it away when he caught her listening to a podcast at midnight.

The bus left the highway and wound its way up a narrow two-lane road, before turning into an empty parking lot surrounded by scraggly trees and a patch of parched grass. Laurelin helped set up the badminton net while the sun beat down, plastering her hair to the back of her neck. But a group of kids snatched up all the rackets before she had a chance to grab one. One of the other girls invited her to play croquet. Laurelin gave her a fake smile and said, "No, thank you." As if she'd be caught dead playing croquet.

She wandered over to the cement picnic table. One of the mothers fussed around it, setting out a heap of food. Laurelin nodded to her and grabbed a water bottle and a turkey sandwich. When she took a bite she almost gagged. Too much mustard. But she was hungry, so she choked down another bite as she walked around the edge of the grass. Gregory, her geeky next-door-neighbor, stood by the badminton net gazing around.

Laurelin ducked behind a tree. It was Gregory's fault she was on this stupid picnic. Or at least his mother's fault, for mentioning it to her dad. Thankfully she'd managed to avoid sitting by him on the bus.

A shady path wound invitingly through the trees. Laurelin waited to make sure Gregory hadn't seen her, then turned to follow it. A breeze toyed with her hair and leaves crunched under her flip-flops. The path meandered, heading mostly south.

When she was bored of walking, Laurelin stopped in a clearing and perched on a boulder to eat the other half of her sandwich. She took a long, cold drink from the water bottle to wash down the mustard. Condensation dripped onto her t-shirt and she shuddered.

Sitting there on the boulder with her back to the path, Laurelin noticed a rocky ridge rising above the trees. She glanced behind her. The path would be easy to find again. If she headed straight west from the ridge she'd run right into it.

A few minutes later, Laurelin stood in the shadow at the base of the ridge. She turned to follow it southward along the edge of the tree line. Sometimes she had to scramble over tumbled rocks, not easy in flip-flops. But she kept going. Even spraining her ankle would be more fun than croquet.

A large oak tree grew right up against the ridge. Laurelin skirted around it, ducking under the heavy, low branches. The ridge veered eastward on the far side of the oak tree, with a narrow gap spanned by a natural stone arch. A raven cawed in the tree behind her, then flew off westward, back toward the path.

Laurelin checked her watch. She'd only been gone twenty minutes, and the bus wouldn't leave for hours. Besides, Laurelin felt drawn to that archway. She ducked under it, pushing through a curtain of hanging roots, and into the sunlight on the other side. Thick, green grass carpeted the small canyon nestled within the rocky ridge. The youth group should have had their picnic here.

Laurelin shivered and rubbed the sudden goosebumps on her arms. In the center of the canyon stood a low, grassy hill with one tree flourishing on the top. The only tree in the canyon. Something about that tree drew her toward it. At first she thought it might be a trick of the light, with the sun blazing down on its lush, green leaves, but she blinked several times and decided it couldn't just be the sun. The tree really did shimmer.

The tree pulled her forward. She had to touch those shimmering green leaves. As she stepped closer to the hill, Laurelin could see white fruit hanging in clusters between the leaves. The fruit smelled heavenly. Her mouth watering, Laurelin began to climb.

Cool grass brushed past her feet, and the summer sun felt good instead of baking hot. But the tree didn't get any closer. Laurelin climbed faster. The hill hadn't looked that high, but somehow she couldn't get to the top of it. Gripping her flip-flops with her toes, she ran up the never-ending hill, her water bottle still clutched in one hand. Even then, she made no progress.

Laurelin collapsed in the grass to catch her breath and rest her aching calves. The shimmering tree stood just above her on the hill, only a few steps away, but no closer than before. She swiveled to gaze down the hill, and gasped.

The hill stretched below her in a gentle slope that went on and on for at least a quarter mile. Laurelin was sitting about half as high as the canyon walls now. She squinted and shaded her eyes, but she couldn't see the archway below her in the canyon. And her watch battery must have died, because its face was blank.

She should head back. Someone might have missed her by now. But then she'd never reach the tree. Laurelin took a drink from her water bottle. She couldn't leave yet. The tree looked so close. She hefted the half-full water bottle and threw it as hard as she could toward the tree. It smacked into the ground beside her feet.

Laurelin picked it up and trudged up the hill. Every few minutes she'd glance over at the canyon walls to gauge how much progress she'd made. The higher she climbed, the further away the walls got, but the tree always stayed a few steps out of reach.

She inhaled. The fruit smelled delicious, like ripe peaches. Or strawberry jam. Or apple pie. Or maybe all those smells mixed together. She'd never smelled anything quite like it. Laurelin's mouth watered. She was almost level with the top of the canyon now.

She jumped when a man stepped out from behind the tree. He wore a white robe and shimmered as much or more than the tree did. Laurelin swallowed. "Hello? What is this place?"

"Hello." His voice was mild, but it resonated through her in a wave of warmth, from the top of her head down to her toes.

"Why can't I get to that tree?" she asked. "I've been

climbing for hours, but I don't get any closer."

He stretched his right hand toward her. "Come."

Laurelin clasped his hand and stepped under the outermost branches of the tree. The man had the most amazing golden-brown eyes. He smiled. Laurelin smiled back, suddenly bursting with a joy she didn't understand. "Thank you."

She gazed up into the tree, dazzled by the brilliance of the white fruit. The intensity of the smell made her dizzy. "Can I have one?" she asked.

"You must complete your mortality before you partake of the fruit," the man said. "But when you do partake of it, it will bring you more joy than you can imagine."

Laurelin choked on her disappointment. "Please?" The smell was beyond resisting. She reached for a piece of fruit, but her hand went right through it. "They're not real?"

"They are real, and they'll be waiting for you."

Laurelin's legs wobbled and she plopped down in the shade of the tree. "So I came all this way for nothing." From the top of the hill, Laurelin could see over the canyon walls. Towering fir trees spread out to the horizon in every direction. The state park was bigger than she'd thought.

The man sat beside her in one graceful movement. "Laurelin, this is not the end of your journey, but the beginning."

"How do you know my name?" she asked, startled. She should be scared right now, since all of this was beyond weird, but the man radiated so much peace that she couldn't feel afraid.

"I've been expecting you," he said. "And since you've never traveled by Tree, I'll teach you how."

"Who are you?"

The man smiled. "I'm the Guardian of the Tree."

"And what do you mean, travel by Tree?"

The Guardian gestured toward the branches above

them. "The leaves are linked to every world in Abba El's universe."

Laurelin tipped her head back and stared at the green leaves rustling in the breeze. "Why does it look so shimmery?"

"This Tree once grew in Earth's First Garden, Laurelin. But when Earth entered its mortal phase, I became the Tree's protector until the children could freely partake of the fruit once more. It shimmers because His hand is upon it, keeping it safe. Though the fruit is forbidden to you for now, the leaves are not. Plucking a leaf allows you to travel to another world, and another Tree."

"Another world?"

"Abba El has more worlds than you can count. And each world has a Tree and a Guardian. You could think of the Tree as a doorway, since all His worlds are connected where the Tree grows on its hill."

"I could travel to another world?" Laurelin grinned, but then her face fell. "How would I get back home?" Her watch was still stopped. Her dad would freak if the bus came back without her, and her little brother would too.

The Guardian placed a hand on her wrist, covering her watch. "Don't worry, Laurelin."

Warmth streamed from the Guardian's hand, filling her with such an abundance of peace that she thought she must be shimmering too. She sat up straighter. "So where can I go?"

"When you travel by Tree, you travel on Abba El's errand, so you go where you're needed."

"I'm needed?"

"Let me tell you a story."

3

Haefen left early the next morning, his leather pack pulling heavily on his shoulders. He didn't begrudge the weight. It would be light enough after his six-day walk to the community on Mount Nevo. The first day of his journey, he followed the Jylboa River upstream. By midmorning on the second day, he was ready to turn his back on the river and head straight south to the mountain.

Haefen left the shelter of the trees and crouched to fill his waterskin before turning to venture across the plains. Just upstream lay the hollow where the river emerged from the base of the Harar Mountains. The plains people believed the hollow to be a sacred spot, but Haefen knew better than to worship a river.

The stone pillars lay half a day ahead. In front of him, the prairie swept along unmarked by anything more than scattered bushes and a few stunted trees in an undulating sea of grass. While Haefen hiked steadily southward, he thought about the Qodesh. He'd been preparing himself for the last four years to enter the sacred Qodesh on Mount Nevo. And now that he'd turned sixteen, it was time.

But his stomach still knotted remembering what his foster father had said. Haefen tugged the paper out of his shirt pocket and read the words again, as he had over and over the day before. "The key you seek...." Could it mean the key to his true name? The traveler must've known he'd want to enter the Qodesh when he turned sixteen, so maybe the key would lead him to his birth father as Rohbert had suggested. But the description of the key wasn't much use. Haefen had no idea what a circle in a circle could be.

Sighing, he folded the paper and tucked it back in his pocket. If he couldn't enter the Qodesh, he'd have to beg the Puerán brothers for their help. Maybe someone in their community would know about his parents. Haefen had prayed morning and night that Abba El would guide his footsteps and lead him to the truth. And he would ask once again when he came to the altar in the midst of the stone pillars.

It was nearing midday when Haefen arrived at the pillars. He had first seen them on the edge of the horizon, barely showing above the prairie grass. For the last hour he'd watched them grow nearer and taller, so that now they stood shoulder-high. He smiled. The last time he'd been here, they'd soared over his head. His stomach growled since he'd eaten no breakfast, but Haefen ignored it. He'd wanted to arrive fasting at the altar so he could feel Abba El's guidance more clearly.

Haefen shrugged off his waterskin and his pack, and set them in the grass beside a pillar. He retrieved the small leather pouch of miriel powder from his pack, and stepped onto the packed dirt in the midst of the pillars. A large stone slab lay alone in the center. Haefen knelt beside it and opened the pouch. He dipped the tip of his right forefinger into the powder and drew a bright yellow spiral on top of the warm altar stone.

He bowed his head and prayed as fervently as he ever had in his life. "Abba El, please. Please guide me. I want to enter the Qodesh to learn more of thee, and to receive a greater portion of thy power." Haefen paused and took a deep breath. "If I need my birth father's name, please help me find it." He opened his eyes and bent forward, pressing his forehead into the powdery spiral. "I ask this in the name of thy son, Ben El, Amen."

Haefen lifted his head, surprised. The warm stone had

been icy cold on his forehead. He stroked the cold center of the smeared spiral with one finger. He ran his hands over the rest of the stone, but it only felt chilly where he'd drawn the spiral. He sat back on his heels and frowned.

Most altars consisted of more than one stone, of course, but the uniqueness of this altar didn't explain how it could feel cold in the midday sun. The riddle intrigued him, and he couldn't let it go. He had to know why it was cold.

Haefen pulled his knife out of the sheath strapped to his thigh and used the haft to dig down into the dirt on one side of the stone. He felt irreverent, disturbing the altar stone, but he also felt driven to unravel the riddle.

The stone had rested in its spot for hundreds of years, but after a few minutes of concentrated digging, Haefen managed to curl both hands under the edge. He straightened his legs from his crouch, and pulled the end of the stone up and out of the dirt. The stone was heavy, but not as thick as Haefen had expected.

Holding up the stone, he crouched back down and peered at its underside. It was encrusted with dirt, but looked like any other stone. But a finger ring rested in the cavity of dirt beneath it. Haefen glanced at the encircling stone pillars. Could this ring be the circle in a circle?

His arms grew tired, and he wasn't sure he could hold the stone up with one hand while he reached for the ring with the other. He closed his eyes. "If this be thy will, I need thy help."

He let go of the stone with his right hand. His breath came in short gasps, and his left arm shook wearily, but he reached in and picked up the ring. He jerked back before the stone crashed into its resting place.

The ring felt ice cold when he first picked it up, but it soon warmed to his touch. How long had it lain under the altar stone? He brushed off the dirt and marveled. An embedded gold thread spiraled its way continuously through the clear metal ring. Haefen had never heard of metal you could see through.

His excitement faded, and he felt uneasy. He still didn't know his birth father's identity. Maybe he should put the ring back. It might not have been meant for him. For all he knew, the Puerán placed a ring beneath every altar.

He set the ring beside him on the dirt and once more hooked his hands under the edge of the stone. He strained to lift it, but he might as well have been struggling to lift a house. Haefen panted with the effort, but the stone refused to budge. He collapsed, defeated, and tried to catch his breath.

He glanced at the altar stone. It would be foolish to set the ring on top of the stone and walk away. Anything might happen to it. Haefen shrugged. He'd ask the brothers about it when he arrived at Mount Nevo. Hopefully they wouldn't be angry that he'd disturbed the altar stone.

Haefen's stomach clenched. Maybe he'd desecrated the altar, and now the brothers wouldn't even let him attempt to enter the Qodesh. He groaned. How could he have been so foolish?

Well, he couldn't change what he'd done, so he'd have to live with the result, whatever it might be. He picked up the pouch of miriel powder and trudged back to his pack. He'd been planning to eat his midday meal here, but he didn't feel hungry any more. He took a long drink from his waterskin, still clutching the ring in one closed hand. Where should he put it for safekeeping?

He opened his hand and stroked the ring. It might fit his third finger, but that was another foolish thought. If removing the holy ring hadn't desecrated the altar, wearing it surely would.

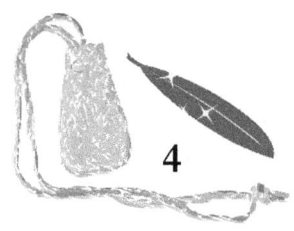

4

The Guardian's warm voice resonated through Laurelin as he spoke. His golden-brown eyes gazed into hers, and through them she could see the things he described. First he told her of a newly created immortal world that Abba El named Piqqeah. And Laurelin saw it.

Piqqeah looked fresh and perfect. It had great forests, vast plains, and all kinds of mountains, rivers, and oceans. Laurelin saw birds and fish, snakes and alligators, and mammals in abundance. She recognized many of them, but others looked like nothing on Earth.

The Guardian told her about Piqqeah's First Garden. A lush array of plants flourished there, and all kinds of animals lived together in peace. Abba El and His son, Ben El, each planted one tree in the Garden as their gift to the new world. The Guardian called Abba El's tree the Knowing Tree, and Ben El's tree the Living Tree.

Laurelin frowned. "But all trees are living."

The Guardian nodded. "Yes, but living is hierarchical. Your mortal life is precious and wonderful, but Abba El's life is of a higher order beyond your comprehension."

Abba El shone like the sun in the image the Guardian showed her. Laurelin pictured him like a superhero, only without the cape.

"Abba El gave the First Garden to two of his children, but evil entered the world. Piqqeah fell from perfection and became mortal." The Guardian grimaced. "Evil destroyed the Knowing Tree and sought to control the world."

The beautiful world faded, its brilliant colors drained. "Why didn't Abba El stop the evil?"

"Abba El, being perfect, couldn't create an imperfect world. But only when Piqqeah became mortal could more of Abba El's children come there to live."

Laurelin saw the two people leave the First Garden. A small village grew from their children, then towns, until finally people lived all over the planet. "But why do you need me to go to Piqqeah?"

"The battle against evil continues," the Guardian said, "and a boy needs your help to overcome it. He will fail without you."

Laurelin saw a boy about her age packing a leather bag. His light brown hair was shoulder length, and he had brilliant blue eyes. He wore sturdy, simple clothes, and smiled happily as he packed. As Laurelin watched, a woman stepped into the room and handed him a blanket. His smile broadened and he said something, but Laurelin couldn't hear him.

"Evil sought to end the boy's life when he was but an infant. But a servant of Abba El saved the child and brought him to the Living Tree in what was left of the First Garden. The Guardian gave them passage to a place the boy could grow up unknown and unknowing."

"The Guardian? So the Living Tree is Piqqeah's Tree on the hill?"

"Yes, the gift of Ben El. The people of Piqqeah call it the Shimmertree."

"The Shimmertree." Laurelin smiled. "I like that."

She should go back to the picnic. They were probably packing up to go home by now, but she couldn't face another sweaty bus ride. And how could she walk away from an adventure like this? She'd kick herself the rest of her life if she left now.

Laurelin stood, and craned her head back to gaze at the bewildering number of leaves. The fruit still smelled heavenly, but then that's what it was, apparently. Hadn't the Guardian said she could eat one when she was dead? Like that made sense. "Which one of these leaves will take me to Piqqeah?" she asked.

"Are you willing to serve, Laurelin? You can go home, or you can go forward."

Home. Home was in California, and she couldn't go back there. "I want to go forward."

The Guardian pulled one of the branches lower and pointed to a leaf no different from the rest. "Then pluck this leaf."

Laurelin grasped the leaf with her right hand and felt life coursing through it. She grinned at the Guardian, and yanked it off the branch.

A blast of cold air sent her reeling. Laurelin whirled around. The canyon had vanished. Towering, snow-covered mountains surrounded the hill instead.

The Shimmertree looked the same, at least. A man stood beside it, dressed in a white robe. He shimmered like the Guardian on Earth, but he had darker hair and eyes of emerald green. He frowned at her bare legs. "Do people on your world walk about half-clothed?"

"Uh, sometimes?"

"Interesting," he said. "Someday you must tell me more of your world. But for now, don't lose the leaf."

His gaze pierced right through her. Laurelin didn't dare ask questions. Shivering in the frigid air, she shoved the leaf into the front pocket of her shorts. She could feel it there against the front of her leg, pulsing with life.

The Guardian stepped forward and placed his hands upon her head. Power streamed into Laurelin, building in strength. Her heart beat faster and she sucked in her breath. And then she was standing next to a strange boy in a circle of stone pillars.

5

Haefen jumped when a girl with long, brown hair appeared out of nowhere. She looked as surprised as he felt, and stared at him open mouthed. He'd never seen a girl wearing short pants instead of a skirt or a dress. Haefen blushed and averted his eyes.

"Where am I?" the girl asked, her voice wavering.

Haefen focused on her face, carefully keeping his eyes from straying to her long, bare legs. "This is the Domarring."

"Domar what?"

"Domarring, the place of the stone pillars," Haefen said, gesturing around them.

"You're the boy. It made sense when I was talking to the Guardian. But I dunno." She shook her head. "This is too weird. Maybe he hypnotized me or something."

Haefen squeezed the ring, still clutched in his hand. Could it be giving him visions?

The girl frowned. "What's that?"

Could an evil spirit be taunting him for desecrating the altar? Haefen took a step back and unthinkingly slipped the ring on his finger. "What do you mean?"

"You have yellow stuff all over your face."

"Oh." Haefen wiped his sleeve across his forehead. "That's miriel powder from praying at the altar." How could he have been so stupid, putting the holy ring on his finger like that? The brothers would be even angrier now.

"Where is this Domar place anyway?"

"These are the Plains of Bicca."

"So the Guardian wasn't lying. I'm not in Missouri any more."

"Missouri?"

"Could I be dreaming?" She sat down suddenly, as though her legs wouldn't hold her up any more. "Maybe I fell and hit my head on a rock. I'm probably lying next to that ridge, bleeding and unconscious."

Haefen stepped closer and crouched beside her. "You're bleeding?"

"What? Are you mental? Who are you anyway?"

"I'm Haefen Ben Rohbert, from the village of Phonteh."

"Are you real, Haefen?" She poked his chest. "You feel real."

Haefen lurched to his feet and stepped back, out of reach. He could still feel the imprint of her finger on his chest. She wasn't an evil spirit, but maybe she was a demon. "What's your name, and the name of your village?"

"Laurelin McCloud, from Pleasant Knoll, Missouri." She reached in her pocket and pulled out a leaf. It rested on her palm, shimmering like a jewel in the sunlight. She poked it with one finger. "This is real at least."

Haefen crouched down to get a closer look. He'd never seen such a leaf before, but he knew where it'd come from. "The Shimmertree," Haefen said. So she wasn't a demon either.

"Yes, the sparkly tree on the hill. The second Guardian put his hands on my head, and then somehow I was here."

"There's only one angel guarding the Tree," Haefen said.

"How do you know? Have you been there?"

"No, the Tree grows far from here. You would journey several weeks just to reach the forest that guards the valley where the hill stands."

"Weeks? Then how do I get back?" She stood and turned in a circle, searching the empty horizon.

"The Shimmertree grows east of here," Haefen said, gesturing, "across the plains, through a swamp and a forest, and across a desert. You couldn't attempt such a journey without supplies." He stared at her strange, flimsy sandals. "And it's doubtful your shoes would survive such a journey."

"Very funny, but I'm not going for a two-week walk. Just have him zap me back, or whatever."

"I don't command the Guardian, Laurelin. You could pray at the altar and ask Abba El for guidance, but otherwise it might be best if you came with me." The brothers on Mount Nevo might know what to do with this strange girl from nowhere, and Haefen couldn't just leave her at the Domarring without food or water.

She peered over his shoulder. "Altar? You mean that rock? Heh, I don't think so." She stooped down and picked a clear container out of the grass. "Here's my water bottle at least." She twisted off the top and took a long drink.

"This is your water container?" Haefen asked, his eyes wide with wonder. "May I hold it?" When Laurelin handed it to him, he turned it around and around in his hands, and squeezed it. It crackled. "Missouri must have many wonders."

"My dad's going to kill me," she said.

Haefen's jaw dropped.

Laurelin laughed. "Not literally. I meant he's going to be upset when he comes to pick me up and I'm not on the bus. Serves him right for making me go in the first place. I wouldn't care, except for my little brother. He'll be worried, too."

"Laurelin, come with me to Mount Nevo and ask the brothers for their help. They might know why the Guardian sent you here."

"Brothers? Are they like the Wizard of Oz? Because I always thought the Good Witch of the North was more helpful." She bumped her heels together several times.

"There's no place like home."

Maybe she really had hit her head. Haefen decided to ignore her babblings. "Are you hungry? I was about to eat my midday meal." He crouched beside his pack and brought out a crust of bread and some vegetables. He offered them to Laurelin, but she shook her head.

"Thanks Haefen, but I'm still recovering from the mustard in my turkey sandwich."

He shrugged away her nonsense. "I can eat while we walk then." It was past midday, and a long way to the stream Rohbert had said to camp at tonight.

Haefen swung his pack onto his back, and they set off across the rippling plains. They hiked for a while in silence. He walked at his usual pace, and was glad to find that Laurelin had no trouble keeping up. Her flimsy shoes, however, might not make it intact to tonight's campsite. Much less three more days crossing the plains, plus one day climbing the mountain.

"Haefen, can I help carry some of your stuff? We could take turns carrying the pack or something."

Haefen smiled. "You're kind to ask, Laurelin, but I'm accustomed to carrying the pack. Tell me about your village instead. Is it in the mountains? Or by the shore?"

"Well, I used to live by the shore, but we moved a couple of weeks ago because of my dad's job. So now we live on the plains, I guess, though not like this," she said, gesturing at the yellowing grass that stretched in every direction.

"How does your father earn his bread?" Haefen asked.

"He's a store manager. The company he works for was opening a store in his hometown, and they offered him more money if he'd move back and get it up and running."

"You don't sound happy about moving."

"No." Laurelin sighed. "My mom died about four years ago, and when we moved it felt like we left her behind. I guess my dad wanted to start over, or get back to his roots, or something. But I liked it better in California."

"I'm sorry about your mother, Laurelin. It must be difficult for you and your father without her."

"Yes, and my little brother. She died right after he was born, so I mostly have to take care of him."

"It's a blessing he has you then," Haefen said. "What kind of goods does your father merchant?"

"All kinds of things. Clothes, gardening stuff, cleaning stuff, stuff for school. Even food."

"It must be a large store."

"Yeah, I guess so," Laurelin said. "So what about you? Where are you from?"

"Phonteh lies on the shore where the Jylboa River flows into the sea. It's a fishing village mostly, though my foster father farms."

"Your foster father?" Laurelin glanced at him.

"Yes, I lost my birth parents as an infant. I'm fortunate, though. My parents have raised me as their own."

After that they walked in a companionable silence. Now and then, tiny, brown birds would fly up out of the grass when they passed. Bees buzzed around the purple spikes of wildflowers, and a breeze caressed his skin. It was a perfect summer's day.

But then he remembered the ring on his finger. What would he do if the Puerán said he'd desecrated the altar? The thought sat heavily in his stomach, mixing queasily with his meal. He should have continued fasting, but it was too late now.

Laurelin squealed and jumped back when a long snake with reddish-brown blotches slithered past her bare toes.

Haefen chuckled. "It's only a milk snake," he said. "Don't be frightened, Laurelin."

"I wasn't," she said. "At least, not much. How do you know we're heading in the right direction? We've been walking for hours."

Haefen smiled. "It's simple. Mount Nevo lies south in a

direct line from the Domarring. All I have to do is keep the afternoon sun shining on my right cheek."

"So, how soon will we get there?"

"We'll come to the brothers at sundown four days from now." Laurelin stopped abruptly, and Haefen turned back to face her.

"What do you mean four days?" Her voice trembled. "Doesn't anyone live in this empty place?"

"The plains people journey with their animals," Haefen said. "But they wouldn't be any help."

"So there's no one closer than these brothers who can help me get back to the Shimmertree?"

"The brothers of the Puerán will be the best ones to advise you if the Guardian sent you to the Domarring."

"Have you ever been to this mountain before?"

"No," he said, "I'm just come of age. I've only ever journeyed as far as the stone pillars before."

"How old are you anyway?"

"Sixteen."

"Heh, me too. So. Four days of hiking across the middle of nowhere. My dad will be ballistic by then. What do you bet he thinks I ran away?" She frowned. "Though I guess I kinda did."

She spoke so strangely. Haefen hoped her head would clear soon. He turned, and they headed south once more.

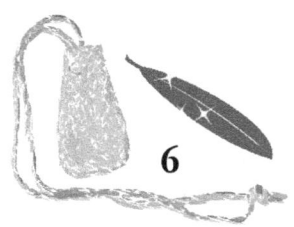

6

Laurelin stole a glance at Haefen when the sun neared the horizon. She had been dying to stop for hours, but she hadn't wanted him to think she was a wimp.

Thankfully, Haefen picked a camping spot at the next stream they came to. It was beside a small grove of oak trees. Laurelin plunked down beside one of the trees and peeled her flip-flops off her grimy, bloody feet.

She'd been building up calluses for a month, but that hadn't been enough for a brisk, five-hour walk. The raw skin burned between the first two toes on both her feet. Plus the flip-flop straps had chafed the tops of her feet with every step, leaving blistered red slashes.

A layer of prairie dust coated Laurelin's legs almost to her knees. She frowned. Her history book last year had had a section about Native Americans dying in droves from European diseases. Open sores coated with Piqqean dust probably weren't a good idea.

She patted the leaf in her pocket. Maybe it granted immunity from strange microbes, along with letting her understand the language. When she'd arrived so abruptly in the stone circle, she had stared at Haefen like an idiot, afraid to say something that would sound like gibberish.

Or if the leaf hadn't helped her speak Piqqean, the Guardian must have done something to make her intelligible and immune. Not much point sending her to a strange planet if she couldn't talk to anyone, and then fell over dead.

Haefen finished clearing the grass from a circle near the

stream. When he'd lined it with rocks, he started a fire, using a tinderbox with deft, sure movements. He walked over to collect more dead wood and saw Laurelin examining her feet. Crouching down, he picked up her left foot. His large, square hands looked brown next to her pale skin. Laurelin flushed and looked away.

"Wash your feet in the stream," Haefen said, drawing her eyes back to his. "I have healing ointment, but first I need to start the evening meal."

"All right." Wow. Haefen's dark blue eyes were over-powering at close range. Laurelin picked up her flip-flops and stepped over to the water. Maybe she should have gone barefoot when her feet first started to hurt, but she'd been afraid to step on something nasty. Like a snake.

It stung something awful when she eased her feet into the stream, though after a bit the cool water felt refreshing. Laurelin rubbed at her legs and her feet, rinsing off as much of the dirt as she could.

Haefen's fire blazed nicely. He unhooked a rabbit from the side of his pack and skinned it while he waited for the fire to burn down to coals.

Laurelin wrinkled her nose. She hadn't realized he had a dead rabbit on his pack. And it'd been hanging there all day, growing bacteria. She was going to have to eat a putrid bunny. Laurelin reached in her pocket and squeezed the leaf. It would be okay. It had to be okay.

She wasn't sure why living in Pleasant Knoll made her crazy, when being stranded on a strange planet with big sores all over her feet didn't. Maybe it was because this was like being dropped inside a book, and nobody in books com-plained about having adventures. Well, except Eustace when he'd ended up in Narnia. But that had turned out in the end, after he wasn't a dragon any more.

Or maybe Haefen had something to do with it. She watched him set a pot of water near the fire to heat. In the meantime, he cut the rabbit meat into small chunks. He dropped them into the pot, then added dried vegetables and ground herbs from his pack, stirred it all up, and put the lid back on. He saw Laurelin watching him and smiled, a heart stopping, crooked smile. Yes, Haefen might have something to do with it.

Haefen gathered up the bones and offal in the rabbit skin, and walked downstream, gazing at the ground. He stopped after a few dozen yards, put the rabbit bits down, and tied a cord to the top of a small sapling. It was too far away for Laurelin to see exactly what he was doing, but he was probably setting a snare. He hadn't planned to have another mouth to feed. But if he caught something every night, maybe they wouldn't run out of food before they got to the mountain.

Haefen washed his hands in the stream and headed back. He checked on his pot, lifting the lid and stirring. Laurelin's stomach growled in spite of herself, and he laughed. "It's nice to know you like my cooking," he said.

Laurelin smiled. "I like the smell at least. I'll give you my final opinion after I've tasted it."

Haefen fished a cloth from his pack and stepped over to where she sat by the stream. He dried her feet, then spread brown, nasty-smelling ointment between her toes and across the tops of her feet. Laurelin studied his bent head while he worked. His hair reminded her of caramel, the mouth-watering kind they sold at the state fair.

Haefen ripped a couple of strips off a piece of thin cloth and wrapped them around and around her feet, tying them in place with loose threads. "Does that feel better?" he asked, glancing up and meeting her eyes.

"Thanks. It feels a lot better."

Haefen smiled. "I'm glad."

His crooked smile was enchanting, turning up more on the right than it did on the left. Laurelin found herself grinning back. She eyed her bandaged feet and wiggled her toes. Her feet did feel better. She wondered what was in the ointment.

Haefen got out his knife and cut through the stitching holding the flap onto the top of his leather pack.

"What are you doing?" she asked.

"Making you some shoes," Haefen said.

Laurelin's mouth fell open. "But you can't ruin your pack."

"It won't harm the pack, Laurelin. And I can put on another flap when I get home."

"Still. I'm sorry I'm such a problem."

"You're not a problem, Laurelin. You're a friend who needs new shoes."

Haefen unlaced the stitching holding the flap in place, then cut the flap into two pieces. He folded one piece in half and had Laurelin stand with her left foot on the leather while he lightly traced around her foot with the point of his knife.

"Thank you, Haefen, for letting me come along and everything."

"It's a good thing you've come with me," Haefen said. "I think it's Abba El's will that we travel together to the Shechinah." He settled himself cross-legged beside the fire and his boiling pot, and fished a fat needle out of his pack. "Tell me a story while I stitch your shoes," he said.

"I just know little kid stories mostly," she said.

"Then tell me a story you'd tell your little brother."

"All right." Laurelin watched him sew up one of the moccasins with his large, capable hands while she told him the story of Goldilocks and the Three Bears. Haefen worked without any wasted movement, as if he made people shoes all the time. Maybe he did. Laurelin studied his shoes, but they looked like real shoes, not moccasins. "So then Goldilocks ran downstairs and out of the house, and the three bears never saw her again."

"I've heard stories with talking animals before," Haefen said, "but never one with animals living in a house. I liked that part a lot, but I don't understand the part about the porridge."

"What do you mean?"

"If Papa Bear's porridge was too hot, and Mama Bear's porridge was too cold, Baby Bear's porridge should have been even colder. It was in a smaller bowl than Mama's, wasn't it? So Baby Bear's porridge should have been too cold, and Mama Bear's porridge should have been just right."

Laurelin frowned. "I dunno. Maybe Mama Bear filled her bowl first, so it had longer to cool."

"Yes, that must be it. When I tell this story, I'll say Mama Bear filled her bowl first." Haefen tied a knot in the cord and cut off the remainder with his knife. "One shoe done." He handed it to Laurelin and laughed. "Tomorrow you can hop on one foot all day. Or maybe I'll stitch your other shoe after our evening meal, if you'll tell me another story."

Laurelin smiled. "I'll tell you the story of the Three Little Pigs."

"A papa, mama, and baby pig?"

"No, they're brothers this time, but they each have their own house."

"More houses? I like your stories."

Haefen lifted the pot off the fire. And when it had cooled, Laurelin took a cautious sip of rabbit soup. It tasted better than she'd expected, and maybe the heat had killed off anything that would make her sick. They shared Haefen's spoon and took turns eating out of the pot.

After their meal, Laurelin scrubbed the pot clean in the stream. Then she told Haefen the story of the Three Little Pigs while he stitched her second moccasin. It was getting dark when Haefen tied a knot in the cord and told her it was finished.

Laurelin put on both moccasins and walked around the campfire. "Thanks, Haefen. These are great."

Haefen had her start clearing the rocks and twigs away from the spot where she planned to sleep. He did the same across from her, on the other side of the campfire. When she was done he handed her a thin blanket from his pack.

"But this is yours. What will you use?"

"My clothes are better suited for sleeping on the ground," he said, nodding toward her bare legs. "I'll sleep fine without the blanket, but you may not."

"Please, Haefen, you don't need to be chivalrous. It's not that cold, and I've slept outside before."

"Chivalrous, what does this word mean?"

They must not have had knights in shining armor on this planet. "Well, it means you don't need to be nice to me, just because I'm a girl."

"I see, but I didn't offer you the blanket because you're a girl, but because your clothes are not as warm as mine, and the night will be cooler."

"Oh. Well, thank you."

"You're welcome, Laurelin," Haefen said.

She wrapped herself in the blanket and lay down on the ground. The stars looked amazing. She'd been camping before, so she knew stars always shone brighter away from civilization, but it was more than that. Maybe Piqqeah was in the milkiest part of the Milky Way. Or maybe this was another galaxy altogether. She grinned. She was on another planet.

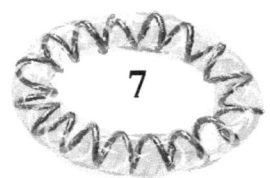

7

Haefen lay down and gazed at the stars clustered above him. Their beauty chased some of the worry from his heart.

Laurelin's stories had been strange. But she told them well, as if she'd had much practice. They'd helped him forget the holy ring and his unknown name for a while. He glanced over to where she lay, but couldn't see her through the fire. She was probably thinking about her little brother. He didn't think her family would be as worried by her absence as she thought. They must know that by visiting the Shimmertree she'd placed her fate in the hands of the Guardian and Abba El. What could be safer than that?

He twisted the holy ring with his thumb and sighed. He'd considered taking it off after their midday meal and stowing it in his pack, but the damage had already been done. And his finger was the safest place for it anyway. Something could happen to his pack, especially now that it had no flap. And what if he lost the ring? How could he face the Puerán brothers then?

He twisted it again. The ring fit his finger so comfortably it might have been made for him. It was strange how it had slipped on so easily, but when he tugged on it, the ring stuck on his knuckle and refused to move past. Well, soap would help it slide off when the time came.

A squeal woke him in the middle of the night, and he jumped to his feet. His snare had caught another rabbit. The fire was a red heap of coals, but he could see Laurelin's outline sit up.

"What was that?" she asked.

"My trap. I'll go check it."

"Wait, I'm coming with you."

She sounded scared, which was silly. But he didn't mind playing the role of protector. "All right. But walk carefully. The moon is thin tonight, and it's easy to misplace a step in the dark."

"But I have this," Laurelin said, and a small light shone from her wrist.

"This is your bracelet?" Haefen asked, stepping closer. "Is it magic?" He swallowed. "You don't come from Asseldam, do you Laurelin?" She had a leaf, of course, but the Sons of Darkness might have learned how to imitate one.

"It's not magic. It's something my dad sells in his store." She took it off and showed him how to press a small button on the side of the bracelet. "Here, you try it."

Haefen took the bracelet and pressed the button several times, watching the light go on and off. "Interesting." Not magic then. At least, not on her world. Haefen handed the bracelet back and walked downstream with Laurelin close behind. The sapling he'd bent over earlier stood upright now. A rabbit dangled from the top of it, held by the cord. "Good, we have dinner for tomorrow." He smiled, though she couldn't see his face in the darkness. "Now let's go back to sleep, or you'll be too tired to walk all day."

Haefen woke first. He washed his face in the stream, then rooted in his pack for their breakfast. Laurelin woke when he knelt to tie the new rabbit onto the side of his pack.

She stretched, then saw what he was doing. "Why would a rabbit go near a trap that smelled like dead rabbit?"

"Because the trap lay near its path to the stream, and it was hungry."

"Rabbits are cannibals?"

"Some kinds are." He handed her a handful of nuts and some dried fruit. "Be sure to fill your water container before we leave. We'll find fewer streams today than yesterday."

When they were ready, they jumped over the stream and continued their hike south across the grassland. Laurelin seemed comfortable in the shoes he'd made her. He dragged his eyes away from her bare legs. Too bad he didn't have a spare pair of pants in his pack.

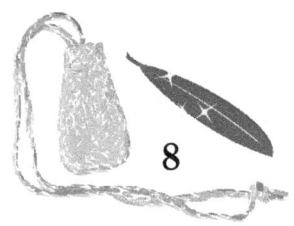

8

That day and the next went by much like the first. Laurelin and Haefen stopped to rest and eat their midday meal, but otherwise they walked ten hours a day. The battery in Laurelin's watch had decided to work again, so she set it for twelve noon when the sun shone directly overhead.

Hopefully she wouldn't have to walk all the way back to the stone circle after she talked to the Puerán people. Her dad would be worried sick by now. He'd probably called all her friends in California searching for her. She'd be grounded for a year by the time she got home.

Why had Piqqeah's Guardian sent her to the circle anyway? She could have met up with Haefen at any point on his trip. After he'd climbed the mountain, even. Maybe the Guardian thought she'd enjoy a five-day walk. When she got back to the Tree she would show him her scabby feet and tell him otherwise.

Laurelin sighed when she woke on the fourth day. Haefen had said they'd reach the swamp today. Yesterday, a squishy, emerald-green plant had gradually replaced the yellowing prairie grass. It squirted juice when she stepped on it. Worse than that were the little gnats that swarmed around their ankles with every step. They had made sure to camp on bare ground last night.

Before they started off each day Haefen checked the sores on her feet, put on more ointment, and re-wrapped them with fresh pieces of cloth. Today, though, he stopped her before she could put her moccasins back on. "Wait," he said.

"We need to grease our shoes to keep the swamp water out."

"Grease?"

Haefen scooped some yellowish goop out of a pouch. "With this. Bear fat mixed with beeswax."

Laurelin wrinkled her nose. "That's disgusting." And she was going to have to touch the stuff with her bare hands.

Haefen laughed at her expression. "I promise, soaking your shoes in swamp water would be worse than rubbing bear fat on the outside of them. Just picture slimy, green water, and insect larvae swirling between your toes."

"Nice. You've talked me into it." She grimaced and scooped out a handful of bear fat. It smelled like old fish, and her stomach roiled. This was worse than eating bunnies every night.

Haefen rubbed the goop on the outside of one of his shoes with a brisk, circular motion. The ring on his finger shone with grease. Laurelin slathered her handful of bear fat onto one of her moccasins and started to rub. It was like oiling her softball glove, only yuckier.

"When we're done with our shoes, we need to wipe some of that ointment on all our exposed skin," Haefen said, pointing to a different pouch.

Laurelin picked up the new pouch with her clean hand and peeked inside. The brownish-green ointment smelled like mouthwash. It might have been all right on its own. But it was nauseating mixed with the fishy-smelling bear fat. "Why do we need this mint stuff?"

"To protect us from the flying insects."

"You realize I'll look like a green clown."

Haefen smiled. "Then we can be clowns together."

When Laurelin's moccasins were as waterproof as they were going to get, Haefen handed her a cloth to clean her hands. She wiped off all the yellow gunk, but her hands still shone with a sheen of grease.

"Maybe you should braid your hair back," Haefen said,

"before you put on the ointment."

"I suppose." Laurelin borrowed Haefen's comb every morning to get the knots out of her hair, but after three long days hiking, and no shower, it hung limply down her back. "I'm not good at braiding, though."

Haefen smiled his crooked smile. "I can help you. I have two little sisters, so I'm good at braiding girls' hair."

"Well, okay," she said, not meeting his eyes. This would be a new experience.

Haefen fished the comb out of his pack and knelt behind Laurelin where she sat cross-legged on the ground. He combed her hair up off her neck and back from her face. She felt his warm breath on her neck as he worked, tugging gently on her scalp as he braided her hair down her back.

"There," he said, tying a leftover piece of cord around the tail of the braid. "Now for the ointment."

Haefen rubbed the greenish ointment on his ankles, though his pants would cover them, and coated his arms liberally before rubbing some on his throat, the back of his neck, his face, and even his ears. He had Laurelin do the same, making sure she coated her legs all the way up, even several inches past where her shorts would cover. He had her turn in a circle so he could see she'd coated all her exposed skin, and had her do the same for him.

"Is this really necessary?" She had the stuff in her hair in spite of the braid, and in her ears too. She could taste it on her lips and her eyes were watering. At least it drowned out the fish smell. She wished she had a mirror to see what she looked like, because Haefen sure looked funny.

"Some of the swamp insects are bloodsuckers and can make you sick," Haefen said. "Others would like to lay their eggs in your skin so their young can feed off your living flesh."

Laurelin cringed. "Couldn't we go around the swamp? I know it would take longer, but that's got to be better than this."

"Avoiding the swamp would add days to the journey in each direction, and we might meet a patrol from Asseldam. The Sons of Darkness keep a jealous lookout for travelers visiting the Puerán on Mount Nevo."

"Sons of Darkness?" Laurelin pictured Boris Karloff lurching around as Frankenstein's monster.

"I don't know if I could protect us."

Protect? So he was serious. "I'm sorry," Laurelin said. "I don't mean to complain. I've just never had to do anything like this before." She waved her green hands.

Haefen smiled where he knelt filling his pack. "As my foster mother would say, tribulations help you grow, so you may as well enjoy them." He stood and swung the pack over his shoulder. "Ready?"

"Sure. Let's go grow, I guess."

But that's when they heard the whistling.

9

At first Haefen hoped it was a bird call, but no bird whistled like that. He turned east to face the sound and saw a man leading a soos in their direction.

Laurelin frowned. "Who's that?"

"A tinker, most likely." The soos bulged even wider than usual from the baskets slung across its back. Haefen had met tinkers a few times. They rarely came to Phonteh, but once Rohbert had taken Haefen with him to Ruomu, on the north coast.

The tinker didn't stop whistling until he'd joined them where they waited. He was an older man with straw-colored hair. His hazel eyes gleamed out of a seamed and weathered face, his skin darkened from years of wandering. The tinker sniffed and looked them over. "Going on a swamp trek then. I'd rather walk around, myself. My name's Patrik."

Haefen nodded. "Hello Patrik." Names had power. Haefen doubted Patrik was the tinker's real name. If it were, he wouldn't have been so quick to give it away.

He glanced at Laurelin, hoping to caution her. But she was oblivious, staring at the soos, wide-eyed.

"Where are you folks from?"

"A village in Shean," Haefen said.

"Shean." Patrik smiled. "I'll be passing through there on my way. Want me to give your family a message?"

"No need. Where are you headed then?"

"Ruomu. If I'm lucky I'll make it in time for the

summer fair." Patrik stroked his greasy beard and glanced toward the south. "You'll be headed to Mount Nevo then."

Haefen stood straighter. Tinkers wandered the length and breadth of Piqqeah, and no one knew where their loyalties lay. "Yes, we're journeying to Mount Nevo. We'd best be off if we're going to make it through the swamp today.

Patrik nodded, but then took Haefen's hand in his, peering at the holy ring. "That's some nice gold inlay. And I've never seen clear metal before."

Haefen slid his hand out of the tinker's grasp. "Is that so?"

"I've never seen a bracelet like that, either," he said to Laurelin. "Maybe you'd like to trade it for a prettier one." He reached into the basket on the left side of the soos. "I have a silver bracelet I found east of the Zarzeef. Paid a lot for it, too."

Haefen took Laurelin's hand and turned her south, away from the nosy tinker. "Not today. Travel safely, Patrik."

Patrik nodded. "Travel safely yourselves."

The tinker was still staring after them when Haefen glanced back a few minutes later.

"That man gave me the creeps," Laurelin said under her breath.

"He disturbed me too. He was too curious for a tinker."

"What kind of animal was that?"

"A soos. You don't have them on your world?"

"Heh, no. If you cut it in half, you might get a water buffalo. Well, if you gave a water buffalo two narwhal horns."

"I don't know these animals, but maybe they live on another continent. They say you can see animals from all over the world in the city of Fusang. I've never been there, but I'd like to go someday."

They trudged along in silence for awhile, and then Laurelin chuckled. "Maybe I should have traded my watch for his silver bracelet. I can always buy another watch when I get home."

Haefen frowned. "You call your bracelet a watch? It watches you?"

"What? No. I don't know why it's called a watch." She thought for a minute. "They should have called it a wrist clock."

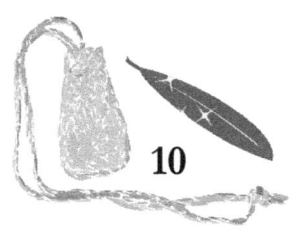

10

More trees dotted the plain the further south Laurelin and Haefen hiked. These weren't the stubby trees she'd seen earlier. They were taller, much taller, with big, round trunks. The new trees almost looked fake. Their branches stuck out at right angles, covered in feathery green needles. Laurelin stroked a few as they passed. The needles felt soft, like cat fur.

Clumps of reeds grew in pockets where the ground dipped down. Laurelin heard more birds than on the previous days, and now and then they saw a squirrel. And once, a big, fat rat. But the most noticeable change was the smell. Something stunk even more than they did. The rotting aroma grew more intense with every step. She took smaller breaths, but it didn't help.

The ground grew uneven. Laurelin stumbled a few times, so she stared at her feet more and the landscape less. The ground cover oozed water around her moccasins with every step. The way it filled in some of the low spots made the ground appear level when it wasn't.

The reeds soon crowded around them, so Haefen took the lead and Laurelin followed. He edged between slimy pools of mucky, green water. The reeds grew thicker and taller until they towered over Laurelin's head. When she brushed by them, they left damp streaks on her green arms and legs.

The pools harbored clouds of insects that rose in a mass when she and Haefen trudged past. Laurelin waved her arms to keep them from buzzing around her head. She wondered which ones were the bloodsuckers, and which ones wanted to lay eggs in her skin. They saw a few swallows eating bugs out of the air, but the swamp could have used some hungry dragonflies. Or bats. Bats could eat five thousand insects a night.

The stagnant pools crowded closer together until they couldn't walk directly south. Haefen weaved back and forth around them. He avoided the slimy, slippery edges, but he lost his balance a few times and ended up down on one knee. Laurelin followed in his footsteps, but she still slipped a time or two. Once she ended up past her ankles in muck. She shuddered while Haefen helped her back to more solid ground, picturing the insect larvae swimming in her moccasins. Waste of time waterproofing them if she kept wading through the swamp.

Midday found them still threading their way through endless reeds and avoiding stagnant pools. After hours of this, Laurelin didn't even feel hungry. The smell from the ointment mixed with the smell of the swamp made a nauseating combination. Instead of eating, they paused and took a long drink.

Laurelin screwed the lid back on her water bottle and watched a brown thrush hop past. "So, how big is this swamp anyway?" She kept her voice light, even though she wanted to grumble.

Haefen shrugged. "We should make it out of the swamp and to the base of Mount Nevo before nightfall, as long as we're still heading in the right direction."

"You mean you're not sure?" Laurelin grimaced and swatted insects away from her face. "Not to complain, but I'd rather not spend the night in here."

"I could hoist you up on my shoulders. By now you'd be able to spot Mount Nevo rising above the reeds." Haefen glanced at her bare legs, then flushed and looked away. "Otherwise we'll figure it out from the sun in an hour or two."

"Hoist me up," Laurelin said. "The sooner we're out of the swamp, the better."

Haefen took off his pack. "Turn around." When she'd turned her back, Haefen grabbed her by the waist, squatted, and stepped under her. He set her down on his shoulders. "See anything?"

He'd lifted her so quickly, Laurelin had been caught off guard. But she steadied herself and shaded her eyes with one hand. Swamp reeds surrounded them like an undulating sea of green. But a cloud-capped mountain rose out of the green a bit to their left. The base of the mountain was barren, but fir trees grew in profusion further up. Granite peaks jutted randomly here and there, like the travel poster on her dentist's wall of Chinese mountains.

She pushed back on Haefen's left shoulder with her free hand. "Turn that way a bit." Haefen shifted. "A little more." He shifted again. "There! Perfect." Laurelin slid off his back and ended up right behind him. His shirt was warm and damp under her hands. She swallowed and moved away.

They started off in the new direction. The humid air was oppressive in the midday heat. Sweat trickled down Laurelin's back, soaking her shirt and the waistband of her shorts. A few loose strands of hair had plastered themselves to her forehead, and she itched all over. With the reeds towering over their heads, even the sunlight looked green and unhealthy. She jumped when a small black crow darted past her face, its belly a flash of purple.

Her head was swimming by the time the slimy pools got further apart. There were fewer reeds. And then the ground finally stopped squishing under her moccasins and turned solid. Laurelin paused and looked up.

A rocky slope stretched ahead of them, growing gradually steeper until it soared straight up to the peak of Mount Nevo. The bottom of the mountain was bare except for a network of small streams cascading down like liquid lace.

Higher up, fir trees blanketed the mountain.

A fresh-smelling breeze tried to ruffle Laurelin's matted hair. The reek of the swamp faded behind them. They'd made it.

11

Haefen waited for Laurelin to catch up. "The worst is over, but we need to hike a bit farther today."

Ointment streaked her face where she'd wiped the sweat out of her eyes. She looked as tired as Haefen felt, but she smiled up at him. "How do you know where to go?"

"My father told me which landmarks to watch for."

Haefen turned and climbed up the slope with Laurelin close behind. The gravel crunched under their feet. He kicked footholds into the shifting hill to keep from skidding. When they topped the slope, they slid a bodylength down into the gully on the far side. That was easier than trying to walk.

A trickle of water meandered through the rocks. They followed the water along the gully bottom until Haefen found the path Rohbert had told him about. It led them up the far side of the gully and into the foothills. Haefen's calves ached, and he wanted nothing more than to sit and lean against a rock. But there'd be time enough for that when they found the campsite.

Laurelin cleared her throat. "How far up the mountain do the brothers live?"

He chuckled. "Don't worry. We won't go as far as that today. It will take most of tomorrow to hike to the Miphtan."

Laurelin hadn't complained, but she must feel even wearier than he did. Thank goodness he'd been the one in the lead all day. It would have been a struggle to stare at Laurelin's back without his eyes wandering where they shouldn't. Especially going uphill.

The first star had already appeared by the time they rounded a corner and found a pool of clear water glimmering in the hollow below. Haefen blessed the travelers who'd dammed the stream generations before. A tendril of water trickled over the top of the dam to splash on the rocks below before weaving its way down the mountainside.

"Would you like to bathe, Laurelin?" Haefen set down his pack and dug around in it for a moment. "Here's soap, and a cloth to scrub off the ointment. I'll go past the next ridge and start our evening meal. I can take my turn when you've finished." He filled the cooking pot with water and left her there, clutching the soap and the cloth in her green hands like he'd given her a great gift.

Haefen climbed over the ridge and found the campsite nestled against the hill, as Rohbert had said. He cleared the fire ring and started a new fire with the stored wood. While he waited for the flames to burn down to coals, he untied the squirrel from the side of his pack and skinned it.

He chuckled thinking about Laurelin's face when she saw the squirrel he'd caught. But all she'd said was she'd never eaten squirrel before. She'd be even more grateful than he would to eat with the Puerán tomorrow night. He put the water on to heat, and added the bits of squirrel meat. Haefen's stomach growled when he tossed the herbs into the pot. It had been a long time since breakfast.

Laurelin climbed over the ridge, scrubbed clean and smiling. She'd had to put her dirty clothes back on, green streaks and all, but her face glowed pink from the scouring she'd given it. Her wet hair dripped on her shirt and she huddled up to the fire, shivering. Haefen handed her his comb.

"Thank you," she said, still smiling. "My bath felt wonderful. Almost as good as a hot shower." She chuckled. "Not sure why I thought I had anything to complain about in Pleasant Knoll."

He grinned. "You're much happier when you're not

green." He stirred the pot one last time. "I'll take my turn now, if you'll keep an eye on our meal."

She frowned at the pot. "Forgot about the squirrel." But she took the spoon.

Haefen gasped when he stepped into the icy water. Laurelin had left him the soap and the cloth. Haefen scrubbed like a madman until he was sure all the green ointment was gone from his skin. He tingled all over by the time he finished, but he felt reborn.

He'd planned to wash out his pants and hang them by the fire, but with Laurelin along he wasn't about to wander around without them. Shivering, he pulled them back on. At least he had a clean shirt. He breathed in the smell of it as he pulled it over his head. It reminded him of home, and of his mother stirring the clothes in her big laundry pot.

He hadn't thought about the sacred Qodesh all day, but as he wrung out the cloth, the ring caught his eye. It had started to feel natural on his finger, but it reminded him that he still didn't know his birth father's name. He twisted the ring and thought about the note the traveler had given his parents. The circle in a circle.

First Haefen would ask the Puerán brothers' forgiveness for disturbing the altar stone, and then he'd show them the note to explain why he'd done such a thing. If he were blessed, they'd know something of his birth parents.

Haefen gazed heavenward. "Please," he whispered, "let me learn my father's name."

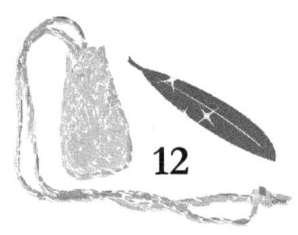

12

The next day dawned cloudy and cold. Haefen had a simmering pot of herb tea to go with their usual breakfast of dried fruit and nuts. Laurelin scooted next to the fire and drank her share with both hands wrapped around the pot. It tasted like licorice.

A stone clattered down the hill and landed beside her. She lurched to her feet, still clutching the pot of tea. "Uh, Haefen?"

"Yes?" He knelt by his pack, but he followed Laurelin's gaze. "A mountain goat. I wondered if we'd see one on our journey."

The goat stood on a tiny ledge and glared down its nose at her. She stuck out her tongue, but the goat didn't move. So Laurelin trudged up to the path and gazed out over the swamp while she finished drinking her tea. Hard to believe it'd been so nasty down there. The swamp looked green and inviting from up here.

She handed Haefen the empty pot when he'd finished smothering the fire. He tucked it into his pack, then picked up a smooth stone and hefted it for a moment before stuffing it in his pocket.

"What's the rock for?" Laurelin asked.

"I want to add it to the kummel."

She frowned. "The what?"

"A heap of stones built by all the travelers to the Puerán."

"Oh, like a cairn." She smiled. "My dad always says 'I'll

put a stone on your cairn' when he says goodbye to a friend. It means 'I won't forget you.'"

"I like that." He smiled. "You could take a stone too, if you want. There are plenty to choose from."

Laurelin chuckled. "True." She found a palm-sized stone next to the path. It would have been perfect for skipping. She stroked it and tucked it into her pocket, the one without the leaf.

The rocky path led them eastward and upward along the mountainside. It was too narrow for them to walk side-by-side, so Laurelin was left staring at Haefen's back, just like the day before.

It took ten minutes of hiking before her legs loosened up and she stopped shivering. It was another half hour before the clouds blew away. Laurelin smiled. After yesterday's misery, they deserved a nicer day for their endless hike across Piqqeah. Of course, now they were climbing straight into the morning sun. She wished she had a pair of sunglasses.

The path curved around the mountain until they were climbing the east face of Mount Nevo. A bit further, and they reached the tree line. Mingled among the fir trees towering over their heads were columnar trees with yellow fruit as big as footballs. The fruit swung in the wind.

"Haefen, do those fruit things ever fall off?"

"What?" He glanced up. "Oh, the seedpods."

"They might land on our heads if the wind picks up."

Haefen chuckled. "Have you never seen a gabo tree before?"

"Nope."

"The soap you used last night was made with gabo oil."

Laurelin eyed the large pods. So that's why the soap had taken forever to lather.

Rock falls covered the path in spots. They scrambled over the debris when they had no room to sidestep around it. Laurelin slipped and lost her balance climbing over one pile of shifting rocks. She yelped and flailed her arms, then found herself hugging the edge of the path. Rocks clattered off the edge and past her feet.

Her heart thudded. She was dangling over a twenty-foot drop. What if she died on Piqqeah? Everyone would think she'd been kidnapped or something. Her dad would never even know what happened to her.

Haefen spun back and grabbed her hand, steadying her and pulling her back onto the path. "Are you all right, Laurelin?" He inspected her. "You've been hurt."

She examined her scraped elbows and her bloody shin, then peeked over the cliff edge beside her. She swallowed. "I'm fine." Her voice sounded shaky, so she cleared her throat. "I'm not lying down there, broken into bits, so I'm fine. But Haefen, next time we go for a hike, remind me to wear hiking boots and better clothes."

He laughed. "Next time I'll find you a soos to ride." He sat on a rock-free part of the path. "Let's rest a minute and catch our breath."

Laurelin settled beside him and dabbed some saliva on her shin. "Haefen, the Guardian wouldn't send me here and then let me die, would he?"

"He's a messenger of Abba El, Laurelin. He wouldn't act without purpose." Haefen chewed on his lip. "I think if we're living our lives the best we know how, we won't die until we're supposed to. All of us have something we need to do before we pass beyond. A life's mission. And if we're working toward it, I think Abba El will let us stay alive until we're finished."

Laurelin frowned. "Then why did my mom die? And babies who die don't have time to do anything."

"Maybe some babies are so pure, their mission is finished when they get a mortal body." He shrugged. "And maybe your mother finished her mission, even though she didn't get to stay and watch you grow."

Laurelin sighed.

Haefen put his arm around her and squeezed her shoulder. "You know you will see her again, don't you?"

Laurelin's eyes flicked to his face. "You think so?"

"Of course. I don't know why sad things happen, but I know death isn't the end. I will see my birth parents in the next life, just like you'll see your mother." He snorted and twisted the ring around his finger. "I suppose that's one way to learn my name."

Just before midday, their path met up with the main path to the Puerán community. It was broad enough for them to walk abreast. No more rock falls, thank goodness. Laurelin glanced at Haefen. He'd put his arm around her. Just for a minute, and just to be nice. But it'd still felt good. She smiled.

The gabo trees had petered out, and the fir trees grew thick and tall on both sides of the new path. Someone had trimmed back trees and branches to keep the path clear.

They stopped to eat their lunch and rest their aching legs. Laurelin's feet ached too. The moccasins had been great hiking across a prairie, but she'd felt every rock she'd stepped on climbing this mountain.

Haefen's pack looked rather empty when he swung it over his shoulder. "We've eaten all your food, haven't we?" she asked, as they resumed their hike. "You won't have enough to get home because of me."

"Not to worry, Laurelin. We'll arrive at the Miphtan before nightfall, and the brothers will give me provisions for the homeward journey."

"What's a Miphtan?"

"The Miphtan is a boundary, or a gateway really, that shields the approach to the Shechinah where the Puerán live. It's the only way in, and those who present themselves at the Miphtan must have pure hearts or the doorkeeper won't let them pass. So, it's also a test."

"How does the doorkeeper know your heart is pure?"

Haefen walked for a few minutes in silence. "I know the doorkeeper can't see the intent of my heart without Abba El's guidance, but other than that I don't know," he said finally.

"Why do you want to present yourself at the Miphtan?" Laurelin asked. "I mean, what does coming to the Puerán do for you that makes it worth traveling so far?" She kicked a fir cone off the path and it disappeared into the mass of greenery.

Haefen glanced at her and smiled. "So many questions. I serve Abba El, as do all my people, and in return he grants us a portion of his power. I come to the Shechinah to enter the Qodesh and learn more of Abba El. I've been preparing to enter the Qodesh for four years. Doing so will grant me a greater portion of his power so that I can return to Phonteh more able to serve my people, and thus Abba El."

Every time he explained something, he used more words that she didn't know. Laurelin fingered the leaf in her pocket. It still beat with life. Some words just didn't translate, then. Like chivalrous. "So, you're going to become a priest, or something, like the brothers?"

"Only in the sense that all the men of Phonteh are priests. We're not able to devote all our lives to Abba El's service. But as we earn our bread and raise our families, we worship Abba El and give him any service he asks of us. Do your people never journey to the Qodesh on your world, Laurelin?"

"No, or at least I've never heard of it before. Maybe we don't have one."

"I find that strange," Haefen said. "I have desired to enter the Qodesh for as long as I can remember."

"So what happens if these brothers don't let me in? You've been preparing for four years, and you said girls don't usually come here. I guess because they don't want to be priests or whatever." She thought about the last big fight she'd had with her dad, the night before she found the Shimmertree. "And you know, my heart might not be pure."

"Laurelin, I believe your heart is pure, or I would not have encouraged you to join me on my journey. I believe the doorkeeper will let you pass. Though," he hesitated and glanced at her wrist, "you may want to remove your bracelet. The Asseldamans are enemies of the brothers, and the brothers may think, as I did at first, that your bracelet comes from the Sons of Darkness."

"Who are they exactly?"

"They're murderers, and enemies of Abba El." He gave Laurelin a quick glance. "If I tell you the story of Asseldam's beginnings, it might help you understand." Haefen gazed into the distance and slowed his pace.

"Once, long ago and far away, in a beautiful land called Betavar, there lived a young king named Beraqel. He was powerful, and kind, and his people loved him dearly. His father before him had also been a good king, and so on, going back many generations, even to our first parents. King Beraqel's people were prosperous, and as the years passed, they built a wonderful city in their land. They built a great castle for their kings, and King Beraqel reigned there in peace.

"But the good king had an uncle, his father's brother, who wanted the kingdom for himself. This uncle betrayed the king." Haefen swallowed. "He slaughtered King Beraqel on the altar, and offered his blood to Heyl El. The uncle sat on the king's throne, slept in the king's bed, and called himself king.

"The uncle was cruel, and the people feared him. Many fled Betavar to save their lives, and left behind the marvelous city and their beautiful land. The uncle had not power to stop them. This enraged him, so he gave his own soul to Heyl El, dredged up the ancient rites, and founded the Sons of Darkness. He changed beautiful Betavar to Asseldam, a fearful land of dark thoughts and sorcery."

Haefen glanced at Laurelin. "My people are among those who fled Betavar hundreds of years ago. They traveled west and north until they came to the sea and could go no farther. That was the beginning of my village of Phonteh."

When Haefen finished the story, they hiked in silence, saving their breath for the journey. The air grew colder the higher they climbed. The sun had crossed over the top of the mountain now, and this face of the mountain lay entirely in shadow. The wind picked up and Laurelin shivered.

"You're cold." Haefen stopped and dug in his pack for the blanket. "Wrap this around yourself," he said, handing it to her. "It'll be warmer when we reach the tunnel and get out of the wind."

His eyes were so blue. "Thanks." She draped the blanket across her shoulders like a shawl and pulled it tight under her chin, covering her bare arms. "How far is it to this tunnel?"

"I'm hoping we reach it an hour before sunset." He shrugged. "But with the sun on the far side of the mountain, I can't see how low it rides in the sky."

Laurelin glanced at her watch. Piqqeah's days were a bit longer than Earth's. Or maybe traveling by Tree had messed with her watch and it wasn't working right. It was about three hours to sunset, though. So two more hours of freezing before they got to the tunnel.

They were a long two hours.

13

Master Long lowered his wooden sword. "Good practice today, Aron." He smiled. "I must be a good teacher."

Aron chuckled and lowered his own sword. "You are the best teacher. Thank you for the extra lesson."

"You are most welcome, though you didn't need one. You're already my best student."

Aron knew it to be true, but it warmed him to hear Master Long say so. "Thank you, sir."

Master Long nodded. "You are dismissed."

Aron bowed and stepped off the practice floor. He slid his wooden sword back into the bin with the others, and grabbed his towel from the hook by the door. He wiped the sweat off his face and neck while he made his way down the hallway to the courtyard door. His stomach rumbled, but it was too early for dinner. It'd been a hard practice. His right arm trembled with fatigue. He massaged the muscle and swung his shoulders to loosen them. A hot bath would be one step closer to heaven.

Aron opened the door to the courtyard and stepped through into the light of the Shechinah. He closed his eyes and lifted his face to the light, letting it wash over him and fill him with peace. Sometimes he took the Shechinah for granted, like all the Puerán must at one time or another. After all, they lived their whole lives in the sign of Ben El's presence.

Aron wished life were as simple as he used to think. All he'd ever had to do was focus on his studies and make his parents proud. But now they expected more than he could give them. They thought he was the one. The living heir of King Beraqel who would drive out the Sons of the Prince Heyl El and reclaim the land of Betavar. He sighed and opened his eyes. No matter how well he did at his studies, no matter how skilled with his sword or his fists, he didn't think Abba El had chosen him for that task.

He crossed the courtyard and swung open the metal gate. His father sat waiting on the bench across the road, in the shade of the apple tree. Aron snorted. Talk of the donkey, and here it comes.

Fredrik jumped to his feet when Aron appeared, and crossed the road to clap his son on the shoulder. "I thought I'd find you here. Walk with me?"

Aron chewed his lip, but he didn't have a good excuse not to. "Just for a bit. I'd really like a bath so I don't offend everyone at dinner."

Fredrik laughed and turned toward the center of the community, maneuvering to walk on Aron's right side so Fredrik's royal blue sleeve showed to advantage. "Is there someone in particular you don't want to offend? Olivia, for example?"

Aron sighed. And so it begins. Not only was he not the heir who would reclaim Betavar, but he wasn't courting the one girl his parents thought worthy to be mother of the next heir in line.

They passed the water clock, and Aron glanced at the time. He'd give his father a few minutes to get whatever it was off his chest, but then Aron was bound and determined to take a scalding hot bath and eat an enormous dinner.

Fredrik strolled along, unhurried, nodding to people they passed. His blue sleeve caught their eye, as it was meant to in a sea of cream-colored tunics and dresses. Fredrik wouldn't want anyone to overlook Beraqel's heir parading through their midst. Aron, on the other hand, avoided wearing a blue-sleeved tunic whenever possible.

"How are your studies?" Fredrik asked.

"Fine, as I'm sure my teachers have told you."

"Yes." Fredrik nodded. "Brother Jonathan told us you're studying architecture now?"

Aron shrugged. "Master Long got me interested. He was describing how different the houses are in his city from the houses in our community."

"It's an excellent course of study. Just think how much help it will be when you rebuild the castle in Betavar."

Aron stopped short. "So shall I go take my bath now?"

"No, no. Just a bit farther and there's a bench where we can sit."

They passed the entrance to the labyrinth. Just beyond its wall of greenery, Fredrik turned down a road with a clear view of the Qodesh. "Here we are," he said, indicating a bench that faced the spiral path.

Aron sat, though his restless hands twisted and untwisted his towel to keep himself from bolting. His father would ask about the Qodesh now.

Fredrik cleared his throat. "So, how soon will you be prepared to enter the Qodesh?"

Aron leaned forward, and watched his toes take turns tapping on the cobblestones. His shoes were scuffed and dirty. He'd better polish them tonight. If his mother saw them at Sabbath service, she'd give him that look he hated. As if his appearance somehow diminished his standing as the heir to King Beraqel. She was as proud of their lineage as his father.

Fredrik tried again. "Word has it that Asseldam is gaining power quickly now, with Ashima standing as High Priest for the Sons of Darkness."

"Sons of the Prince."

"Don't use that name here," Fredrik said through his teeth, gesturing to the Qodesh above them.

"That's their name," Aron said, slowly and distinctly. "Why equivocate? Besides, Ashima's changed his name to

Mahan, now that he's no longer a Puerán."

"Ashima, Mahan, that doesn't matter. But don't give evil a name."

"Whatever."

"Aron, why do you fight your destiny?"

"You don't know I'll be the one for whom the crystal chest will open." Aron met his father's gaze. "No matter how much you wish for it to happen, it will open when Abba El decrees, and not before."

Fredrik shook his head. "You don't understand. With Mahan as High Priest, the good must rise to keep the Sons' power in check. This is the time when the king's breastplate must be claimed to protect the rest of the world from their creeping rot. They're like a spot of mold that must be cut out before it corrupts everything around it. Who will unite the Khaznians, Fusang, Ruomu, and even the Taph, if not us? As the king's direct heirs, this is the time we've been waiting for these hundreds of years."

"You're making assumptions. Mahan can't use the power of Abba El to achieve Heyl El's desires."

Fredrik slapped his hand over Aron's mouth. "Are you tempting my forbearance, or Abba El's? Don't name the evil one. Names have power, or didn't you learn that when you were knee high? Were you as reluctant at your lessons then as you are now?"

Aron bristled. "You know I'm at the top of my class."

"Then why, in the name of all that is holy, will you not enter the Qodesh and claim King Beraqel's breastplate from the crystal chest?"

Aron couldn't tolerate another moment of Fredrik's lofty expectations. He surged to his feet, his fists clenching and unclenching as the words boiled out of him. "Because when I stand in front of the crystal chest, staring at it like an idiot, it will remain closed. As it did for you, and your father, and so on, all the way back to when the widowed queen placed the breastplate inside the chest, shut the lid, and spoke the prophecy. That's why, Father."

Aron stalked off. If he hurried, he could still fit in a bath before dinner.

14

Haefen was shivering almost as much as Laurelin. He turned up his shirt collar, stuffed his hands in his pockets, and trudged up the path with his chin tucked into his chest. But the wind was brutal, and nothing helped.

Laurelin's legs were blue with cold, so Haefen fished his filthy shirt out of his pack and had her put it on. It was much too big. The sleeves hung past her fingertips, and the tail of the shirt hid her short pants so that it looked like she had nothing on underneath. Haefen would have blushed if his face hadn't been frozen.

Laurelin wrapped the blanket around her waist like a skirt to shield her legs from the frigid air. The wind whipped the blanket around like a mad thing as they hiked on. Laurelin clutched the blanket with white knuckles, holding it in place. Maybe she wasn't any warmer, but Haefen didn't know what else to do.

For the last half hour, the left edge of the path had skirted the top of a cliff. The rock crumbled if they stepped too close. So he and Laurelin hugged the right side of the path, ducking beneath the waving fir tree branches that threatened to knock them off the path.

By the time they reached the tunnel, they were exhausted from fighting the wind. Haefen's muscles ached with every upward step. Especially his calves. Laurelin had to be even more tired, though she hadn't complained. Not that they'd been able to talk with the wind roaring past.

Ducking into the tunnel opening was like climbing out of a riptide. The tunnel turned, then turned again, and then once more, before opening into a wider thoroughfare. The turns blocked the wind from following them inside. Haefen and Laurelin stopped and grinned at one another. The relief was glorious.

"We made it!" Laurelin said.

"Yes." Haefen stretched. His muscles ached from tensing against the wind. "No one in Phonteh ever described such a fierce wind on their journey to the Puerán. I'm sorry Laurelin."

"It's not your fault. Thanks for loaning me your shirt."

"Sorry about the smell."

She laughed. "The wind took care of that."

They pressed on, following the tunnel as it ascended the side of the mountain. Every so often, large windows had been cut into the rock on the left side of the tunnel. The Puerán had glassed in the windows with thick sheets of clear crystal. The crystal magnified the view, so that the plains below seemed only a stone's throw away.

When they paused at the first window, Laurelin stroked it, wide-eyed. "A telescopic window. I've never seen anything like it."

"Neither have I." Haefen knocked on it with his fist. "I wish I could stay longer and learn all the Puerán know."

The tunnel was strange too. It was a perfect square, two bodylengths tall, and just as wide. But the rock had no tool marks, as if the tunnel had been melted into the rock instead of chiseled out of it.

They trudged upward in silence, too weary to talk. The light was fading, each window illuminating less than the one before. They reached the end of the tunnel an hour later, turning, turning, and then turning again before stepping out into the twilight. The first stars had begun to appear, and the air was cold but still.

"This is it?" Laurelin spun in a circle, gazing up at the surrounding rock walls.

They stood in a square hollow. Opposite the tunnel exit, the western wall rose twice as high as the others, a blank rock face soaring ten bodylengths into the darkening sky. The kummel nestled against the foot of the southern wall. The rocky pile was as tall as Haefen. He fished the stone out of his pocket and stepped closer to add it to the heap. Laurelin did the same, reaching up to set hers at eye level, and patting it into place.

"So, what now?" she asked. "Where's the doorkeeper?" She eyed the rocky walls. "Actually, where's the door?"

"The Miphtan has no door."

"A doorkeeper with no door? How do you get in?"

"If the doorkeeper finds you pure, he takes your hand and invites you in."

"Through a tunnel?"

"Through the rock."

Laurelin frowned. "That doesn't make sense." She stepped closer to the western wall and ran her hands across the smooth surface of the rock. She chuckled. "Should we wait for the thrush to knock? Though the setting sun can't show us a keyhole."

Laurelin was babbling again. She hadn't done it for days, but maybe her fatigue had brought it on. Haefen rubbed his damp palms on the side of his pants. He dropped his pack and knelt on the gravel with his arms folded behind his back. He bowed his head. "The doorkeeper will tell us when to approach, Laurelin. For now, we wait."

"Okay." Laurelin paused. "Should I kneel like that too?"

"It's a sign of my willing submission. You shouldn't join me unless you're willing to submit to anything the doorkeeper asks of you."

"Maybe we should have talked about this before we got here." Laurelin knelt beside Haefen, wincing as the gravel dug into her knees.

Haefen had debated for days whether he should tell Laurelin how to enter the Miphtan. But he wouldn't have been able to explain the burning without making her afraid, so he'd decided to let her experience it for herself. The doorkeeper would recognize her innocence in spite of her ignorance.

"He's not going to ask me to jump off a cliff or anything, is he?"

Haefen chuckled. "No. He won't ask anything that Abba El would not also ask." He glanced over at her. "Hold your elbows behind your back."

Haefen breathed deeply, but his heart still raced in his chest. He didn't know what he'd do if his foster father's name weren't enough to enter the Miphtan. After a long, hungry journey back to Phonteh, he'd arrive disgraced. They would think he'd been unworthy. Well, his family wouldn't, but the rest of the village would. What else could they think?

Laurelin shifted uneasily beside him. "Are you sure there isn't a bell to ring or something? How will anyone know we're out here?"

"The doorkeeper will know," Haefen said.

Minutes passed in silence. Laurelin sat back on her heels and sighed. Haefen focused on his breathing.

A voice rang out in the stillness. "Who comes prepared to face the challenge of the Miphtan?"

Haefen stood and hoisted his pack. "Laurelin, watch what I do and listen to what I say. Then you'll know what to do when it's your turn." He stepped closer and placed his right palm flush against the western wall. He flinched when the ring chimed against the rock. "I am Haefen Ben Rohbert from the village of Phonteh." His voice bounced off the cliff face. "I accept the challenge of the Miphtan."

He heard Laurelin rise to her feet behind him. Still pressing his hand against the rock, Haefen chanted:

"I stand prepared at the holy place,

My heart is pure and my desire strong.
Grant me entrance to the sacred mountain.
In the name of Ben El, lay your hands upon me.
Let me learn in the light of the Shechinah.
Let me ascend the path to the Qodesh."

The rock warmed under his fingers and his hand sunk under the surface, as it should. The relief left him weak. At least Rohbert's name was enough for this.

Then a wave of heat surged through his hand and up his arm. The burning reached his shoulder, and in an instant, shot up to his head and down to his feet. Haefen felt exhilarated. His heart threatened to burst with the wave of joy that washed over him. He opened his eyes and blinked away tears.

The rock closed over his wrist, and a voice said in his mind, "Come." It was a mild voice, almost a whisper, but that one word resonated through him, body and spirit. Haefen stepped forward into the rock and left Laurelin alone in the hollow.

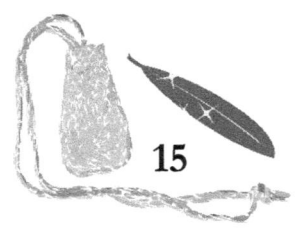

15

Laurelin fought back the panic. Yes, Haefen had walked through a rock wall. But she was on a different planet, for goodness sake. That was crazier than aligning the empty spaces in his atoms, or whatever it was Haefen had done. Only, she was going to have to do it too. Or else be stuck out here. In the dark. With no food.

Maybe the doorkeeper was in charge of aligning the atoms. She'd watched like Haefen had told her to. All he'd done was stick his hand on the wall, say stuff, and get sucked in. She could do that.

Laurelin knelt back down and waited for the voice. Was someone watching her right now, through a peephole or something? That could be how the doorkeeper knew she and Haefen had knelt there, all submissive.

Her knees hurt. She wiggled her shoulders, but her arms felt awkward and strained folded behind her back. It started to drizzle and Laurelin gave up. She stood and rubbed her knees, then hugged her aching arms to herself.

The voice rang out a second time. "Who comes prepared to face the challenge of the Miphtan?"

Here we go. Laurelin faced the wall and put her right palm flat against the rock. The wall was warm under her cold fingers. "I am Laurelin McCloud, from Pleasant Knoll," she paused, "on the planet Earth." That should give the doorkeeper a shock. "I accept the challenge of the Miphtan."

She didn't remember how the next part was supposed to go, but she did her best. "I stand here at the holy place, with a pure heart and, uh...." Her mind went blank. "And I was wondering if you'd let me come to your sacred mountain. I'm sorry, I don't remember what else I'm supposed to say."

Laurelin waited, but nothing happened. She must have failed the challenge. She shivered. If the doorkeeper didn't let her in, she didn't know what to do. She was wet and cold, she didn't have a way to light a fire, and she didn't have any food. Haefen had left her with nothing but a blanket. He could at least have left his pack. Though, now that she thought about it, she didn't know how to use his tinderbox or set a snare.

Laurelin's hand sank into the wall and the rock beneath her hand burned. A wave of heat surged past her wrist and up to her elbow, burning through her flesh and into the bone. She yanked at her hand, but she was trapped, glued to the rock.

Her heart pounded in her ears. She was going to die. The burning reached her shoulder, and then shot up to her head and down to her feet. Haefen had left her here to die. She tried to cry out, but she had no voice. And her face was melting. No, those were tears streaming down her face.

She didn't know if the burning lasted minutes or hours. While her body burned, her mind flicked through all her memories. She saw her mother holding her above the waves, walking on the beach, kindergarten. She saw her parents bringing Benjamin home from the hospital. He'd been so tiny, but he'd held onto her finger and wouldn't let go. She saw her mother's grave, and she shouted at her father while tears streamed down his face.

Her life was flashing before her eyes, just like everyone said it would. She was dying, and she'd hardly lived. And her dad would think she hated him enough to run away. She sobbed against the wall and would have fallen, but the rock still gripped her tight.

When she'd lost all hope, the burning drained down and out of her body, leaving her trembling and exhausted. She opened her eyes. Her right hand was still embedded in the rock. A voice in her mind whispered, "Come." The voice pierced her heart, and her despair became a surge of joy. She took a step and watched her leg vanish into the rock. She held her breath and took a bigger step.

A wizened old man in cream-colored robes held her by her right hand. He smiled, his brown eyes twinkling in his lined face, and released her. "Welcome to the sacred mountain, Laurelin McCloud. My name is Brother Sigurd."

"Hello." Laurelin's voice was shaky. She cleared her throat and gazed around the stone hallway where she and Brother Sigurd stood. The hallway stretched off in both directions as far as she could see. Stone lined the walls, the floor, and the ceiling, just like the tunnel with the telescopic windows. Haefen was nowhere around.

"Haefen has gone onward," Brother Sigurd said. "You can rejoin him soon." He handed her a cream-colored handkerchief.

Laurelin blew her nose and wiped her eyes. "Thank you. And thanks for letting me in."

"Your heart is pure, Laurelin. You are most welcome here." He gestured to some cushioned chairs on the far side of the hallway. "Rest a moment."

Laurelin sank into a chair, her legs shaking with fatigue, and stared at the wall she'd just walked through. It was seamless, with no sign of where she'd entered. She had walked through a rock wall.

Brother Sigurd perched on the chair beside her. "You must be weary. Such a long journey you've had." He smiled and patted her knee. "Let me know when you're ready to go on."

Laurelin sat in a stupor. She didn't think she'd ever want to leave the cushy chair and the sweet, old man. But then her stomach rumbled. She blushed. "Could I get something to eat?"

Brother Sigurd chuckled. "Of course. Haefen's waiting

for you in the dining hall."

Laurelin followed Brother Sigurd down the long hall-way. There weren't any lamps or light fixtures, but the hallway glowed with a soft, bubble of light that followed them as they walked.

They passed closed doors on both sides of the stone hallway, door after door after door, until Laurelin lost count. None of the doors had any markings, and Brother Sigurd never paused.

Just when Laurelin thought the hallway would never end, a pair of massive wooden doors gleamed in the distance. They filled the end of the hallway from wall-to-wall and floor-to-ceiling, dark and pitted with age. But despite their massive size, the doors swung open easily at Brother Sigurd's touch. Laurelin stepped through into a clearing.

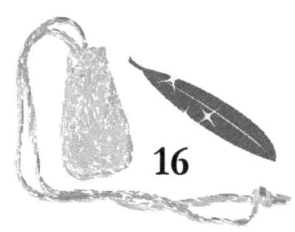

She turned to say goodbye to Brother Sigurd, but he was gone, and so were the doors. Enormous beech trees surrounded the clearing instead, with broad trunks and intertwining branches.

It should have been dark by now, but light shone down through leaves that trembled in a breeze. Laurelin couldn't see the sun, though, and the light was different. Clearer maybe, and whiter.

A building stood on the far side of the clearing, hidden in vines except for the open door. The dining hall. Enticing aromas drew her closer, and her stomach rumbled again. A murmur of voices greeted her when she stepped into the doorway.

The hall was lined with empty tables, except for where Haefen sat behind a dirty plate. A group of people surrounded him, laughing and chatting like old friends. His traveling clothes were grimy compared to the Puerán in their cream-colored robes.

Laurelin fingered her stained clothes and ran her fingers through her ratty hair. Embarrassing. She would have unwound the blanket from around her waist, but a woman had already seen her. She stepped toward Laurelin, smiling in welcome. Her faded brown hair had been pulled back into one long braid that hung down her back.

"You must be Laurelin," she said. "I'm Sister Nora. Come join us and have your evening meal." She chuckled. "Haefen has eaten one meal already, but I think he'd gladly eat another."

She drew Laurelin into the hall and over to Haefen's table. A man offered Laurelin his chair, and someone set a plate of steaming food in front of her.

"Thank you," Laurelin said. It was awkward, eating in front of a bunch of strangers. For all she knew, her Earth table manners were rude on Piqqeah. But while Haefen chatted, Laurelin took a bite of a green, mashed vegetable. It was sweeter and more flavorful than mashed potatoes. The first green forkful melted in her mouth, and suddenly she was ravenous. She speared a bite of tender chicken and savored the familiar taste. So much better than squirrel and rabbit.

Laurelin took a roll from a basket while Sister Nora poured her a cup of sparkling juice. It smelled like straw-berries. "Tell us of your land," she said.

Laurelin sipped the juice while she thought about what to say. Should she tell them she came from another planet? She set down her cup and smiled. "I'm from Pleasant Knoll, in North America."

"North America." Sister Nora shook her head. "I've never heard of it. Is it across the sea from Ruomu? Do many people live there?"

Ruomu? "We have a lot of cities."

"Do you have any castles?" one man asked.

Laurelin shrugged. "There's one called Hearst Castle." Probably not the kind of castle the man meant.

An older man, with long, white hair, stood and addressed the group. "That's enough for tonight. The travelers are tired. Let's find them some beds, and we can hear more on the morrow." His voice was kind, but rang with authority. Laurelin smiled. The man looked like Gandalf.

The group said goodnight and filed out of the dining hall, though Sister Nora and one of the men stayed, talking quietly near the kitchen. Laurelin ate faster now that she was out of the limelight. She finished off the green vegetable and spread butter on her roll. She moaned when she took a bite. "Bread. I didn't realize how much I missed it."

Haefen chuckled and took a roll for himself. "I knew you'd like their food better than mine. And your heart was pure, as I said."

"Yeah, about that. It would have been nice if you'd given me a warning about the whole burning rock thing."

"Yes, I'm sorry if it took you by surprise, Laurelin."

She snorted. "Surprise is an understatement."

"Five days wasn't long enough to prepare you. If I'd told you of the fire, you might have feared it too much to make an attempt."

"Why did you get to step through the wall after a couple of minutes? It took me forever."

Haefen shrugged. "The cleansing fire is different for everyone. Your heart is like no one else's."

Cleansing fire. Interesting. Laurelin finished off her chicken, then frowned. "Why did you say your name was Haefen Ben Rohbert? I know Rohbert's the name of your foster father, so is Ben your middle name?"

Haefen smiled. "No, Haefen Ben Rohbert means Haefen, son of Rohbert."

"But you're not really the son of Rohbert."

"I know." Haefen picked up his cup and turned it in his hands. "I don't know the name of my father. I told you my parents died when I was an infant, but I don't know who they were. Two travelers carried me to Phonteh, an old man and a girl. His granddaughter maybe. They'd found me crying at a campsite, and said both my parents were dead."

Haefen set down the cup and met Laurelin's gaze. "The sickness had taken many in Phonteh, including Rohbert and Rute's two sons, so they were kind enough to take me in."

"That must have been hard, growing up not knowing who you were."

"Yes, but my foster family loved me like their own. My

name wouldn't matter, except Rohbert thinks I might not be able to enter the Qodesh without my birth father's name."

"The Qodesh? You mean, the whole reason you came to Mount Nevo?"

Haefen twisted the ring around his finger. "Yes. But I'll talk to Brother Efrat tomorrow and see what he says."

So that's what had been eating him off and on during their trek. A long way to go if you didn't know you'd get in. "Who's Brother Efrat?"

"The leader of the Puerán. He's the one that sent everyone away just now."

"Gandalf. Right." Laurelin yawned.

"You're tired."

Haefen retrieved his pack from where it leaned against the wall, and Laurelin followed him over to where Sister Nora and the man waited. "Goodnight, Haefen," Laurelin said.

"Rest well, Laurelin." Haefen turned to follow the man through a set of double doors.

It was silly, but Laurelin felt lost, watching him walk away. She followed Sister Nora out of the dining hall and down a path to a long, low building. The sky was still light. Laurelin checked her watch, which she'd tucked into her pocket. It was after ten o'clock at night. Why wasn't it dark?

Sister Nora opened the door of the low building and stepped inside. Laurelin followed behind. Beds stood perpendicular to the two long walls, with a corridor running down the middle. A small dresser stood beside each bed. Most of the beds were occupied, but Sister Nora tiptoed to the far end of the building where a bed stood neatly made up and empty. She opened the top drawer of the dresser beside it and pulled out a nightgown.

"This should fit you," Sister Nora said softly. "This bed is reserved for guests, so you may use it for as long as you choose to stay. In the morning, ask the other girls where to wash. They'll be excited to meet a new guest." She smiled. "I just hope they allow you to sleep until you're fully rested."

"Thank you, Sister Nora."

"You are most welcome, Laurelin. May your stay be long and fruitful."

Sister Nora left, and Laurelin kicked off her moccasins and undressed. She pulled the nightgown over her head and was about to climb into bed, when she remembered the leaf and her watch. The nightgown didn't have any pockets. The top drawer of the dresser was empty, but she found a handkerchief the next drawer down.

She pulled her watch out of her shorts' pocket, and fished out the leaf. It was as fresh and alive as the moment she'd plucked it from the Shimmertree. She stroked it once before she set it with her watch in the center of the handkerchief. Then she tied the corners of the handkerchief into a knot and tucked it under her pillow.

Laurelin crawled into the bed and stretched out. The bed felt wonderful after sleeping on the ground for four nights. Five days she'd been gone now. Her dad must be frantic. And Benjamin. Laurelin sighed. Who was taking care of him while their dad was at work? Her eyes were too heavy for her to worry long, though. She rolled over and fell fast asleep.

17

Haefen awoke with a jerk, covered in cold sweat. The light of the Shechinah streamed through the small window on the opposite wall, but it couldn't erase the last image of his dream. Brother Efrat had loomed over Haefen, taller than life, and shouted, "You shall remain nameless forevermore!" Nameless. That was the price he'd paid for disturbing an altar stone and putting on the ring.

But it'd been a dream. His fears coming to life while he slept. It wasn't real. Yet Haefen's stomach still roiled, as if his dinner planned to make a reappearance.

Everyone else still slept. Haefen dug in the dresser beside his bed and found a clean tunic and pants. He crept out of the dormitory, carrying his shoes, and stepped into the nearby bath house. He'd scrub himself clean and go confess to Brother Efrat. If he hurried, he might catch him before Sabbath service began.

Clean and damp, Haefen poked his head into the dining hall and knocked on doors, until he found Brother Efrat in his office. It was a plain little room, except for the large painting hanging on the wall behind the desk.

One of the other brothers interrupted before Brother Efrat even had a chance to sit down. He excused himself and stepped out into the hallway, so Haefen studied the painting.

It depicted Ben El in a white robe, like other paintings in the community. In the one near Haefen's dormitory bed, Ben El sat cross-legged on the grass and talked with the child perched on his lap. In one of the dining hall paintings, Ben El knelt and gazed into a sky so bright, he might have been gazing into the sun.

The painting in Brother Efrat's office depicted Ben El kneeling on a grassy hill with the root ball of a small sapling cupped in his dirt-stained hands. In front of him, a small mound of dirt sat beside a hole. Ben El was about to plant the Shimmertree. Even in the painting, the leaves trembled with life, like Laurelin's leaf. Haefen leaned closer. How had the painter achieved such a believable illusion?

Brother Efrat shut the door behind him. "You like the painting?"

"The artist has great talent."

Brother Efrat nodded. "I find myself staring at it at least once a day. Now," he said, scooting his chair closer to Haefen's, "what troubles you?"

Haefen smiled bleakly and held out his right hand. The ring sat snug as ever on his finger. "I found this ring beneath the altar stone at the Domarring, and I fear I committed sacrilege by disturbing the altar and removing the ring. I didn't mean to put it on my finger. And once I'd put it on, I couldn't remove it."

Brother Efrat leaned back in his chair and rubbed his chin. "Haefen, why did you lift the altar stone?"

"The stone felt.... I was praying at the altar, and when I sealed my prayer in Ben El's name, the stone felt cold beneath my forehead. I wasn't thinking clearly, my heart sat so heavy in my chest, so I lifted the stone to see how it could feel cold in the noonday sun."

"And?"

"And I saw the ring resting in a hollow beneath the stone. I thought...." Haefen sighed. "I thought it might be the answer to my prayer, though I realize now that's foolish. But in any case, I took the ring from under the altar. And when I regretted my actions, I no longer had the strength to lift the stone. I suppose Abba El didn't want me to think I could hide my wrongdoing by replacing the ring."

Brother Efrat frowned.

"Anyway, I'm sorry I disturbed the altar stone." Haefen tugged on the ring, trying once more to remove it. The ring wouldn't budge. "I'm sure I can remove it with soap," he said at last. His knuckle was red and sore from his efforts.

Brother Efrat held out his hand. "Allow me."

Haefen rested his hand in Brother Efrat's. With the forefinger of his other hand, Brother Efrat tapped the ring and murmured something under his breath. The ring slid off Haefen's finger and into Brother Efrat's palm. Haefen gaped.

Brother Efrat peered at the golden spiral while turning the clear ring round and round between his fingers. "Why did you think the ring was an answer to your prayer?"

Haefen took the folded square of paper from his pocket. "I desire with all my heart to enter the Qodesh, but I don't know my father's name." He stroked the paper. "When I was a baby, a stranger gave this paper to my foster father when he agreed to take me in."

Brother Efrat set the ring on his desk and took the paper. "The circle in a circle. I see." He refolded the paper and handed it back.

"Haefen, you haven't desecrated the altar. I don't know why this ring rested beneath the altar stone, or how long it may have lain there. I've read of a similar ring in the histories we brought from Betavar, though. I'll see if I can find the reference while you're here. How long did you intend to study with us before approaching the Qodesh?"

"A week. I was well tutored in Phonteh."

"Well then, I won't dawdle in my research. Wear the ring in the meantime," he said, holding it out to Haefen. "Its presence may alert you to why it chose you."

"Chose me?"

"Yes. That's obvious, at least."

Haefen slid the ring back onto the third finger of his right hand, where it sat as snugly as it ever had.

"About your father's name. There is some precedent for using a foster father's name."

Haefen held his breath.

"Though the circumstances were rather different. It was soon after we founded our community, and some chose to renounce fathers who had joined the Sons of the Prince in Betavar-that-was."

"They entered the Qodesh using their foster fathers' names?"

"Yes. But, I doubt your father was a Son of Darkness. Do you understand why your name is so important?"

"It's who I am. My heritage and my birthright."

"Yes, and even if your foster father is a good man, he's not your heritage. When you speak your true name at the Qodesh, the elements will recognize you ever after. They will obey your voice when you command them in the name of Ben El, as I did with the ring. If you can't command the elements, you can't receive more of Abba El's power, so you have no reason to enter the Qodesh. Your name is a watchword. A key."

Haefen's heart ached. "Then I've journeyed here in vain."

"No." Brother Efrat drummed his fingers on the desk. "I believe the ring was an answer to your prayer, as you thought. Let me seek for the reference I mentioned."

Maybe he still had a chance. "Thank you, Brother Efrat."

When Haefen rose to take his leave, Brother Efrat stood as well and rested his hand on Haefen's shoulder. "Do you know of the labyrinth?"

"Yes. Many men of Phonteh tell of it, though only a few ventured to walk its spiraling path."

"Do you know the difference between our labyrinth and

a maze?"

"Yes, one man in Phonteh grows a corn maze each year, and at harvest time the children race to find the correct path to the center. But the labyrinth has only one path."

"Yes, a maze is a puzzle to be solved, but the labyrinth has only one choice: to enter or not. Its path represents the path of our lives, and those who choose to walk it learn to see themselves through Abba El's eyes as they spiral toward the center. Spiraling withershins on the outward journey expands their view of mortality and eternity."

Brother Efrat squeezed Haefen's shoulder. "Perhaps you should take the time to walk the labyrinth. It might help you find the answer you seek." He smiled. "But now it's time for Sabbath service."

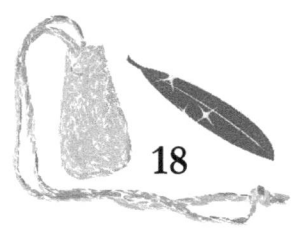

18

"Sister Nora said her name is Laurelin," someone whispered.

Laurelin had been dreaming about running up the Shimmertree hill. Not the one on Earth, but the Piqqean hill, surrounded by those steep, snow-covered mountains. Her face was buried in her pillow when she awoke, and at first she thought she was in her own bed. But then she remembered, and sat up with a start.

Teenage girls in cream-colored nightgowns surrounded her bed. Laurelin slid one hand under her pillow and fingered the pulsing leaf through the handkerchief.

"I'm sorry. We didn't mean to wake you," one of the older girls said. She had thick blonde hair that hung in a wavy curtain to her waist. "We see girl visitors so seldom. My name is Olivia."

"Hi." It was awkward to have all those eyes focused on her.

Olivia must have sensed this, because she shooed the other girls away. "Go on now. If you don't hurry you won't be ready in time for worship. Today is our Sabbath," she said, turning to Laurelin. "Would you like me to show you where to wash?"

"Please. I feel completely grody." Laurelin tucked her ratty hair behind one ear and slid out of bed, still clutching the knotted handkerchief. "Do you know what happened to my clothes?"

"We put them in the laundry. But we have clothes you

can use while you stay with us. If you'd like."

Laurelin grinned. "Thank you." Even if her own clothes had been clean, they would have looked stupid compared to what everyone else was wearing.

"Then I'll show you the baths."

The warm bath felt luxurious after the cold pool she'd bathed in at the base of the mountain. Though the soap wasn't any better. When she was clean and dry, Olivia handed Laurelin a cream-colored cotton dress that hung to her knees.

After a quick breakfast, Laurelin hurried beside Olivia to the community's place of worship. "Thanks for showing me around."

Olivia smiled. "As I said, we have few girl visitors. You're the first during my time as head novice, so I'm privileged to be your escort."

"What kind of novice?" The wide path they followed cut through a grassy field. A whole crowd of people was headed in the same direction.

"The novices train to become Iysha, or sisters of wisdom. The Shechinah is the place of the brothers of the Puerán, but it is also the place of the sisters."

"So it's not just a guy thing. What do novices do?"

"We're taught the stewardships of women from a young age. But as novices, we enter the service of Abba El and learn the mysteries of women."

Ahead of them, a large, domed building glinted in the sunlight. People approached it from four directions along diagonal paths that cut through a field of short-clipped grass. "This is the House of Light," Olivia said.

Doors stood open around the perimeter of the House, so that the approaching crowd could enter without delay. Laurelin filed in after Olivia and found herself in a large amphitheater. Tiers of seats around the perimeter sank gradually down to a circular floor at the bottom. Olivia and Laurelin climbed halfway down a set of steps and found two seats next to the aisle.

While she waited for something to happen, Laurelin gazed around the building. With the tiered seats and domed roof, she might have been sitting in a giant ball. Light shone down through the seamless crystal dome so that it sparkled like a diamond.

A stone table stood on the central floor below, bathed in the light from the crystal dome. The table was strange. The base was just a pile of irregular chunks of rock, and then a large, crooked stone slab lay across the top of this pile to form the tabletop.

While more people trickled down the stairs, Laurelin estimated how many seats there were. About twenty-four hundred, if she'd done the math right. Though the topmost tier wasn't individual seats, but benches that ran along the length of each section. Like nosebleed seats in a stadium.

The sections tapered, so that the bottom tier of seats had only two seats in each section. Old men filled half of them, and old women the other half. One of them was the old man from last night. Gandalf, or whatever his name was. Just as she spotted him, he rose from his seat and stood beside the stone table. The people had been talking softly amongst themselves, but they quieted now and gave him their full attention.

Laurelin wasn't sure what she'd expected, but the worship meeting turned out to be a lot of singing, some talking (both men and women), and a few prayers. The talks were interesting, but the announcements made no sense. Olivia had given her a leather bag to hang from her belt, and that's where Laurelin had tucked the knotted handkerchief. She patted it now and then, wishing the leaf could explain the words that didn't translate.

Even though she didn't understand all of it, Laurelin was happy she'd come. An incredible feeling of peace filled the House of Light. It soothed away her worry about getting home, and reminded her of the peace she'd felt with the Guardian. He'd told her not to worry. Something would work out.

Laurelin hunted for Haefen during the service. Families filled most of the tiers. The tier she was on had more girls than the others. Novices, probably. She spotted Haefen up on nosebleed row, packed in with other boys his age. He must have felt her gaze, because he glanced over and smiled, then gave her a small wave. Laurelin smiled back. It was nice to know she wasn't alone with two thousand strangers.

After the last prayer, the old people in the bottom tier rose first and ascended the steps. Some of them were quite frail. The rest of the people waited respectfully for them to pass their tier before they also rose and filed up the stairs and out of the building.

One of the old men ascending the steps beside Olivia and Laurelin was more frail than most. He held onto his companion's arm and paused every few steps to catch his breath. He happened to pause on the step just below them, and glanced their way. "Laurelin!" he said in some surprise.

"Er, yes," Laurelin said. "Hi."

"You look just the same."

Other people turned to see what the old man was staring at. Laurelin blushed.

His companion urged him upward. "Come Brother Jeffree. The people are waiting."

"Yes, yes of course." Brother Jeffree shook his head as if to clear it, then continued his slow walk up the steps.

Laurelin and Olivia rose with the rest of their tier and waited for the people from the lower tiers to pass, before they too filed into the aisle and ascended the steps.

"That was weird," Laurelin said, as she and Olivia followed the path back through the field.

"You mean Brother Jeffree?"

"Yes. How did he know who I was?"

Olivia chuckled. "He probably knew who you weren't."

"What do you mean?"

"Everyone in the community knows everyone else. Because he didn't recognize you, he must have realized you were the girl visitor everyone's been talking about."

"Oh." Laurelin thought for a minute. "Then what did he mean that I looked just the same?"

Olivia shrugged. "He may have been wandering in his mind, Laurelin. I wouldn't worry too much about it."

"Okay." They walked for a while in silence. "Oh, I wanted to ask you, why didn't it get dark last night? And even now I can't see the sun." Laurelin gestured to the sky above them. "It's cloudy, but it's so bright."

Olivia smiled. "That's the Shechinah."

"Haefen talked about the Shechinah, but I didn't know what he meant."

"It's the sign of the Presence of Ben El. His protection. As long as we're worthy, he'll watch over us. That's why we're sometimes called the Children of Light."

"Does the light come from somewhere in particular?"

Olivia hesitated. "No, though it shines brightest near the Qodesh because that's his house."

"Ben El lives in the Qodesh?"

"Not in the sense you mean, Laurelin. He doesn't sleep or eat there, but it's kept sacred to him so that he may visit and give us counsel. Only his watchful care stays with us always."

"So, this cloud thing is always there? You've never seen the sun? Or stars?"

Olivia smiled. "I've seen stars. When I was a child, our leaders often led us through the Miphtan to camp on the mountainside. They wanted us to see what life is like outside the Presence." Her face grew wistful. "It was strange the first time I saw the sky grow dark. We lay on our blankets and watched the stars appear, one by one, like jewels." She shook her head. "Abba El has so many creations, more than I could ever count."

"So you know about other worlds?" Laurelin asked.

"Oh, yes. Many people on Piqqeah came from other worlds originally. Also, before I became a novice, I spent a full day alone on the mountainside while I prepared myself to pass through the Miphtan without help. It was a glorious sight to lie there alone in the dark and see the sky in all its majesty."

Laurelin followed Olivia into the dormitory. "What do you mean you passed through the Miphtan without any help?" They sat facing one another on Olivia's bed.

"Brother Sigurd didn't guide my steps as he had when I was a child."

Laurelin stared. "You mean, you just walked right through the rock wall?" She never would have made it if Brother Sigurd hadn't taken her hand.

Olivia laughed at Laurelin's expression. "Yes. When my training as a novice is complete, I'll try to enter the Qodesh in the same way. Though entering the Qodesh will be more difficult than passing through the Miphtan."

"You have to walk through a rock wall to get into the Qodesh?"

"Yes. There's no other way."

"No hidden door? And no one helps you?"

Olivia shook her head. "It's the holy place. Only the pure can enter the house of Ben El."

The rest of the day was uneventful. It was heaven to sit around talking instead of hiking all day. As she lay in bed that night, Laurelin stared at the ceiling and wondered what Benjamin was doing. He probably hadn't brushed his teeth since she'd left. It's not like their dad would remember to remind him. Did they miss her? She frowned. It was hard not to worry about getting home.

Laurelin rolled over and snuggled into her pillow. She would miss Haefen when she made it back to Earth. Actually, she missed him already. Besides catching that glimpse of him in the House of Light, she hadn't seen him since the night before. He was probably busy getting ready for his walk into the Qodesh. Would she ever see him again after he entered the Qodesh? She'd feel cheated if she didn't.

With that thought, she drifted off to sleep.

19

Aron waited for the House of Light to empty, before sliding off the bench and ducking out the nearest door. It made no sense that apprentices had to wait for everyone to leave, while novices didn't.

The path was clogged with people chatting, as always. But his blue-sleeved tunic caught their eye, so everyone smiled and stepped aside to let him pass. Aron smiled his thanks, though he longed to yank off his tunic and trample the blue sleeve into the dirt.

But his mother expected him to arrive home properly clothed as soon as Sabbath service ended. And if he didn't, he'd get another lecture on his glorious heritage and his expected future.

Aron smiled. The best part of a day at home was seeing his little sister, Qanaah. He could feel the present he'd made her rubbing against his shin with every step.

Aron had spent days carving and painting a wooden replica of King Beraqel's sword. The legends said Queen Elin escaped from Betavar with the sword strapped to her leg, though it vanished soon after. Qanaah had always loved the story of the sword. She wanted to be the one to find the lost treasure.

Aron trudged along the path to the north side of the community where the houses lined up in rows. Their house was at the end of the farthest row, nestled up against the edge of the plateau. It had been passed down in their family since the settlers built it for Queen Elin. Legend said she liked to pace along the edge of the plateau, gazing northward to watch for her husband's approach.

That made no sense, of course. By the time the queen arrived at Mount Nevo, her husband was dead, slaughtered by the Sons of the Prince. And even if he weren't, he'd come from the east, not the north. Still, Qanaah thought the king's sword might be hidden along the edge of the plateau. She'd searched among all the rocks, and dug holes all over the garden before she gave up.

Aron opened the door and called out, "I'm home."

Qanaah came running, rushing from her room like a small whirlwind. She buried her face in his tunic and gave him a tight hug. "I missed you."

Aron laughed. "Missed me? You saw me yesterday."

"But you left before the midday meal."

"Well, I spent most of the day finishing your present."

"My present?"

Aron raised an eyebrow. "Aren't you having a name's day this week?"

"Yes!" Qanaah danced from foot to foot, her pigtails flying. "I don't have to wait, do I? I won't see you till next Saturday. Please, Aron, don't make me wait."

"I'm sorry, Qanaah. You can see I don't have it with me. Unless...maybe I put it in my pocket." He patted his pockets. "Not there. But wait." He rolled up his pant leg.

Qanaah squealed. "You found the sword?"

"Silly, King Beraqel's sword wasn't made out of wood." He unstrapped it from his shin and held it out to Qanaah with both hands. "My lady, your sword. May it serve you well."

"Thank you, thank you, thank you." Qanaah grabbed it and swung it over her head. "This is the best present ever."

The rest of the Sabbath went downhill from there. His mother looked exhausted and didn't say much. His father was polite enough during the meal. But after he and Aron cleared the table, he took Aron aside and browbeat him about the

Qodesh.

"A new boy came through the Miphtan Saturday night. He's only planning to study a week before his attempt to enter the Qodesh. You could enter with him next Sabbath." Fredrik droned on, explaining how fortunate it all was.

Aron wished the boy every blessing, but he didn't want to enter the Qodesh next Sabbath. Thankfully, Brother Efrat came knocking and interrupted them, inviting his father outside. Aron watched them for a while through the window, strolling back and forth, deep in conversation.

But it was too nice to last. Fredrik burst back into the house and dragged Aron into his office. "It's been found. Or at least we think so."

"The sword?"

"What? No, the ring. King Beraqel's ring." Fredrik sank into his cushioned chair. "That boy who just arrived. Haefen's his name. He found the ring. Efrat is keeping it quiet until he's searched the histories, but he thought we might have a family legend that would help him recognize it."

"So if you're supposed to keep it quiet, why are you telling me?"

Fredrik frowned. "Isn't that obvious? The ring will be yours once I'm gone."

"If it is the king's ring. Where did he find it?"

"Under an altar, of all places." Fredrik grunted. "I don't see how he'll enter the Qodesh after a stunt like that."

He glared at Aron. "And of course it's the king's ring. How many rings could match the description, with such fine workmanship? The metal is clear, for one thing. And Efrat said the gold inlay was flawless, as if it'd been set there by the finger of Ben El."

"You didn't see it? Haefen didn't give it to Brother Efrat?"

Fredrik shook his head, his mouth grim. "The boy's wearing it, if you can believe it. But once Efrat confirms it's the king's, we'll tear it off his finger. Maybe you should talk to this boy, Aron. Explain the situation. Maybe he doesn't realize he's overstepped himself. How about this. Get the ring from the boy, and I'll let you wear it for your Qodesh attempt."

Aron frowned. His father would never leave him alone. "I'll think about it."

20

When Haefen had finished his breakfast, Brother Efrat took him to find Brother Biorn, his tutor for the week.

"He doesn't eat in your dining hall," Brother Efrat explained as they trekked to the western side of the community. "But you may have noticed him at Sabbath service."

Haefen doubted it. Seeing that large a throng gathered in the House of Light had been overwhelming. And he hadn't noticed anyone in particular. Except Laurelin.

The community was laid out in a grid. Cobblestone paths and rows of fruit trees separated blocks of buildings into areas with a similar purpose. The southern portion of the community was devoted to learning. Brother Efrat pointed out classrooms for the different age groups, libraries, study halls, debate centers, and so on. Even a school of combat techniques.

Haefen frowned. "Combat?" The community seemed too peaceful, too protected, to worry about war.

Brother Efrat nodded. "Yes. We've always had such a school. You'll have heard of the battles our people fought before they abandoned Betavar and fled for their lives. Next time we won't flee."

"Next time? No matter what happens anywhere else, the Puerán will be safe here in the Shechinah."

"We wouldn't abandon the rest of the world. And the light of his Presence only protects our community if we're worthy. If we allow our behavior to slip and decay, if we turn away from Ben El, the Shechinah will leave us."

"But the Qodesh is here."

"The entrance to the Qodesh. The Qodesh itself is cupped in his hand. If he removes the Shechinah, he'll remove the Qodesh as well."

Haefen's mind spun. He'd always thought of the Children of Light as part of the mountain they lived on. Firm, unchanging, immovable.

As they approached the far edge of the community, the buildings became smaller and farther apart. Like small stone cottages, really, that wouldn't have been out of place in Phonteh.

Brother Efrat led Haefen to one of these cottages, opened the door and gestured for him to enter. Inside was a single room, square and unfurnished. A man, Brother Biorn presumably, sat cross-legged on a braided rug in the center of the wooden floor, his hands on his knees and his head bowed.

Haefen expected Brother Efrat to introduce them, but he lifted a hand in farewell and shut the door. Haefen didn't want to disturb Brother Biorn either. He sat across from him and waited, fascinated by Brother Biorn's hair. It hung in a blond braid over his shoulder, so long that it lay heaped on the floor beside him.

Brother Biorn opened his eyes and smiled to see him sitting there. "Hello, Haefen."

His calm voice relaxed a knot in Haefen's stomach. "Good morning, Brother Biorn."

"Have you spent much time in meditation before?"

"A little." As little as possible, Haefen could have said.

"You've read in The Book of the Faithful that we need an open heart and a willing mind to understand the mysteries of Abba El. Do you know what this means?"

Haefen shrugged. "That we humble ourselves and turn our lives over to him? And we need pure thoughts and sincere desires."

"Yes. Join me now in meditation. Focus on opening your heart and your mind to his will."

Haefen bowed his head and closed his eyes. He fought to focus his thoughts like Brother Biorn had said, but they wandered around like loose chickens. He'd drag them back, refocus, and they'd wander off again.

He wondered if he should walk the labyrinth. He wondered what Laurelin was doing right now. He thought about his father's name. That reminded him of the ring and he twisted it on his finger. His stomach gurgled and he wondered how long it was until the midday meal.

A few minutes later Brother Biorn said, "Good."

Haefen opened his eyes.

"It can be difficult to focus your thoughts. But without a sharp focus, you'll struggle to perform the rites that mark the end of your apprenticeship. And the stone wall into the Qodesh will remain impermeable. So that will be our task for today."

Haefen caught his breath. Would they sit around meditating until dinner time?

But instead, Brother Biorn stood and showed him how to stretch. Haefen stretched his fingers out toward the walls, mirroring Brother Biorn. They held them shoulder high until Haefen's arms trembled.

"Breathe. Deeply. In through your nose and out through your mouth." Standing, his braid almost reached his knees.

Next, Brother Biorn had him lie on his back and stretch his fingers toward the wall behind him, while at the same time stretching his pointed toes toward the opposite wall.

"Breathe, Haefen. That's it. Slow, deep breaths, in and out."

Lastly, he had Haefen lie with his hands by his sides and tense every muscle in his body. Brother Biorn counted slowly to fifty while Haefen breathed in and out through his clenched teeth.

"Now, let it all go," Brother Biorn said. "Relax all your muscles from your head to your feet. From your arms to your legs. From your throat to your back. Good."

Brother Biorn knelt beside him and placed one forefinger on Haefen's forehead, and another on his chest.

"Close your eyes now, Haefen. Breathe in and out, long and deep. Focus on your mind and your heart. Open them. Feel them expand. Feel the peace that comes when you allow your will to align with his."

Haefen did feel peaceful. It washed over him in a wave. He focused on it, reveling in it. Warmth poured into his body. Light filled him. He smiled, and then sighed.

"Good."

Haefen opened his eyes when Brother Biorn removed his fingers. He sat up, and they faced each other, cross-legged on the rug.

"That's the peace you're seeking when you meditate, Haefen. It doesn't always come." He flicked his braid over his shoulder. "But it'll come easier when you learn to focus your thoughts."

"May I ask you a question?"

"Of course."

"How long have you been growing your hair?"

Brother Biorn chuckled. "The brothers shaved my head ten years ago when I prepared to ascend to the Qodesh, as they will yours. I decided to let it grow after that as a sign of my covenant with Abba El, and my willingness to consecrate my life to him."

"So, you're never going to cut it?"

"No, I'll cut it soon, when I become a full priest of the Puerán."

"But you didn't have to do that, to become a priest. Did you?"

Brother Biorn smiled. "No, I chose to." He stood and

took a copy of The Book of the Faithful from a shelf near the door, flipping through it while he sat back down. "Here," he said, handing it to Haefen. "Study the words of the prophet Kehunnah before it's time for our midday meal. Pay particular attention to this section," he said, pointing, "where he talks about trusting in Ben El. Remember to keep your mind and your heart open. One way Abba El speaks to us is through sacred writings."

Brother Biorn brought Haefen his midday meal. They ate together in the empty room, discussing the passages he'd read. When they'd finished eating, Brother Biorn talked about order and chaos, contrasting the power of the servants of Abba El with that of the Sons of Darkness.

"They seek for prestige, Haefen, building it on the fear of their followers. They wish to dominate, to accumulate. They reign by force, and offer signs and deceptions as proof of their worthiness to lead. The few in power manipulate and deceive the many who aren't, so that they can glut themselves on their people's labors. What is the result, Haefen?"

"Well, people fear them. And their land is always in an uproar. And," Haefen racked his brain, "they imprison or enslave anyone who disagrees with them."

"Yes, Asseldam is a land of chaos and decay. The god of their land is Heyl El, the god of fear. They honor him by spilling the blood of their people. Even slaughtering innocent children on their polluted altars."

Haefen shuddered, picturing a blood-soaked altar crowned with the body of one of his sisters.

"In contrast, our service to Abba El brings us joy and growth. Any power we have comes from our honor, and our leaders guide us in harmony with our will. That's evident by the peace in our land and the peace in our hearts. Instead of striving to accumulate more wealth than another, we strive to be more useful to our neighbors and our god. Our service glorifies his name, and our land flourishes."

Brother Biorn pulled a small, rough stone out of his pocket and placed it on the rug between them. "I found this on my way to the kitchen. Haefen, by the power of your honor, and the power of your mind, move this stone."

"You mean, not touching it?"

"You remember the story of Hanoch in The Book of the Faithful?

"Yes." That was one of Haefen's favorite stories.

"Hanoch commanded the elements to come to the defense of his people, moving rivers and mountains by the power of Abba El." Brother Biorn raised one eyebrow. "Is that a true story?"

Haefen nodded. "Yes."

"So you believe the power of Abba El contains the power to command the elements in the name of Ben El?"

Haefen had watched Brother Efrat command his ring, so he didn't doubt the Puerán had the power. Though, a ring wasn't a mountain. "Yes, his power can command the elements. If there's need."

"Observe the stone." Brother Biorn gestured to his right, and the stone moved a handwidth in that direction. He gestured to his left, and the stone moved back.

Haefen gaped, and then swallowed hard, looking from the stone up to Brother Biorn's face. He'd never seen anyone in Phonteh do that.

"It matters not to the power of Abba El whether it's a mountain or a stone." He smiled. "But since there's no need to move Mount Nevo today, we'll start with the stone. Tell me Haefen, how was Piqqeah created?"

"By the voice of Ben El. He commanded the elements and they came together, organizing themselves according to his word."

"Yes, the elements obeyed his voice. So if you command the elements in the name of Ben El, then by his grace, they will obey." Brother Biorn rose to his feet and swung his braid back over his shoulder. "I'll leave you to practice, Haefen. I'll return an hour before dinner."

When he'd left, Haefen stared at the stone. It was one thing to believe it was possible, and even to watch someone do it. It was another thing to do it himself.

He worked to focus his mind and his heart, then gestured with his hand the way Brother Biorn had. He willed the stone to move in the name of Ben El. It didn't.

He refocused himself and tried again. And again. Haefen knelt and bowed his head, pouring his heart out and praying for the power. Praying to be worthy of the power.

He tried again. He was still trying when Brother Biorn came back hours later, though the only time the stone had moved was when Haefen picked it up to see if it were stuck to the rug. Sweat plastered his tunic to his back, and his head ached. But he had accomplished nothing.

Brother Biorn gave Haefen a hand up, then held him by his shoulders and gazed into his eyes. "You know it's possible, Haefen. But you must know it's possible for you." Still holding him by one shoulder, Brother Biorn tapped Haefen's chest with a forefinger. "You must know here. But," he said, releasing him, "tomorrow is another day."

Haefen followed him out the door and into the light of the Presence. Brother Biorn turned to walk beside him on the cobblestone path. "I'll take you to the apprentice demonstration in the amphitheater, Haefen. It'll take your mind off the day and let you relax before dinner."

21

The dormitory was empty when Laurelin awoke. She put on the dress from the day before, and tugged the leather bag out from under her pillow. The leaf was as green as ever. It pulsed between her fingers, shimmering in the light streaming through the window.

They'd made it to Mount Nevo so Haefen could do his Qodesh thing. But what was she supposed to do? She'd promised the Guardian she'd help Haefen fight against evil. She remembered that moment so clearly, with the Guardian standing in front of her, shimmering like the leaf. She hadn't worried about her family. Or how she'd get back to Earth.

Laurelin was worried now. Benjamin would be lost without her. But, Haefen was staying the rest of the week on Mount Nevo. So, she'd stay here too. That creepy tinker, Patrik, had been the only evil thing on the way here. And there couldn't be anything evil among the Puerán. So something bad must be going to happen on Haefen's trip back home. And she'd help him battle it, if she could. Then hopefully, she could go home. Laurelin tucked the leaf back in the bag with her watch.

She spotted Sister Nora eating breakfast in the crowded dining hall, so she took her plate of food over and sat beside her. "Good morning."

Sister Nora smiled. "Good morning, Laurelin. I hope you slept well."

"I guess I overslept, since all the other girls were gone when I woke up."

"Yes, they must be up early to perform their duties."

Laurelin ate a piece of green melon. She didn't know why, but everything tasted better on Piqqeah. "Sister Nora, is it all right if I stay here the rest of the week?"

"Stay as long as you desire, Laurelin. You're always welcome here."

"Thanks. While I'm here, I know I'm not a novice or anything, but could I help with something? Like, wash dishes, or sweep the floors? I don't know, whatever the community needs."

"Good idea. When serving others we refine ourselves." She smiled. "It'll also give you something to do while the other girls are busy."

"True." Laurelin finished her melon and took a bite of scrambled eggs. "Do you know what Haefen's doing today?"

"He'll be with his tutor all day. He has a lot to learn before his attempt to enter the Qodesh." Sister Nora wiped her mouth on her napkin and pushed her chair away from the table. "I know someone who could use your help, Laurelin. Have you finished your meal?"

"Sure." Laurelin followed Sister Nora out of the dining hall and down a cobblestone path to the far western side of the community. It was a long walk. The buildings were small and square on this side, like the cities she made out of blocks for Benjamin to play with. Mini houses alternated with large gardens, with mini streets running between them.

Some of the buildings they passed must have been workshops. Hammering sounds came through the open windows, as well as the sound of laughter. Everyone sure was happy here.

Sister Nora passed by all the gardens and other buildings, and headed for a lone hut on the far side of the mini city. Smoke billowed out of its chimney, though the day was warm. The hut was set well away from any other structures, near rounded granite peaks that jutted around the edge of the plateau.

Something stank. And the closer they got to the hut, the worse it smelled. Laurelin plugged her nose.

Sister Nora laughed. "You'll get used to the smell if you're brave enough to stay. This is the tannery, Laurelin. Come in and I'll introduce you to Brother Udi, our tanner."

She stepped inside the open doorway, and Laurelin trailed after. Light and air filtered into the building through slatted walls and the open door and windows. A large, square man bent over a tabletop where he scraped at a stretched skin with a metal tool.

"Hello, Brother Udi."

"Sister Nora," he said, turning toward them. His dark hair stuck up in spikes, like he'd been running his grimy hands through it. "What brings you to my realm?"

"This is Laurelin, Brother Udi. I know you've been short on help, so I thought you might find her useful."

Brother Udi put down his tool and wiped his hands on a small towel. "Hello, Laurelin. I'd love some help." He grinned. "I don't know why, but all my assistants run away as soon as I turn my back. Are you sure you won't mind spending your day here?"

Tanning had to be more interesting than washing dishes and sweeping floors. She smiled. "I'm sure."

Sister Nora put a hand on Laurelin's shoulder. "I'll leave you to it. Enjoy your day."

When she'd gone, Laurelin stroked a stack of finished hides. "So, you turn skins into leather?"

"Yes," Brother Udi said. "I take smelly animal skins and turn them into beautifully soft leather."

"It's the animal skins that stink?"

Brother Udi chuckled. "That and a few other things. Come and I'll show you."

Laurelin followed Brother Udi out a back door and into a courtyard crammed with large, open-topped barrels. The barrels were filled with liquid in various colors, from a muddy brown, to orange and bright red. Hides soaked in every barrel. The smell was more acrid out here. It caught in Laurelin's throat and made her cough.

A stream ran beyond the courtyard, curling along the jutting peaks. Only a few stunted trees grew nearby. They probably didn't like the smell either.

Brother Udi explained how he first scraped the flesh off the animal hides with a blade, and then soaked them for three days in water and wood ash. After that, he wrung out the hides and scraped the hair off. "Here's a hairy goat hide waiting just for you," he said, picking one off a stack.

Back inside he handed Laurelin a scraper and set her to work scraping off the hair. He went back to the hide he'd been working on earlier, scraping gobs of rotting meat off the hide and onto the table. "When you've removed all the hair Laurelin, we'll tan your hide in a mixture of brains, water, and a dollop of fat."

Laurelin wrinkled her nose. "Did you say brains?"

Brother Udi laughed. "Yes. As a gift to tanners, Abba El gave every animal just enough brains to tan its own hide."

22

Haefen wasn't sure what to expect at an apprentice demonstration. Brother Biorn had left him at the bottom of the amphitheater steps. The stage was at ground level, and semi-circular tiers had been carved into the granite hills guarding the southern edge of the plateau.

He hesitated, wondering where to sit. People milled around on the stone tiers, talking and joking. It was awkward not to know anyone. But then Haefen spotted Viktor from his dormitory, near the center of the crowd, and climbed the steps to join him on his tier.

Viktor grinned when he saw Haefen. "You look weary. I'm dreading my last weeks of apprenticeship."

"Do you know everything apprentices do during that time?" After a day spent failing to move a stone, the next five days stretched out like an eternity. "What do the brothers expect of us?"

Viktor shrugged. "It's not something we speak of, though everyone drags around exhausted. But at the end, their countenances glow like the Shechinah."

Two groups of apprentices had formed on the stage below them. The group on the left surrounded a boy wearing a tunic with one blue sleeve. "Who's that?" Haefen asked, pointing him out to Viktor.

Viktor lowered his voice. "That's the one and only Aron, heir to the throne. And those are his loyal flatterers."

"To the throne? You mean a descendant of King Ber-aqel?"

"Not any descendant, but the oldest son of the oldest son, and so on, back to the king. Though Beraqel's oldest son was killed, of course. So I should say the oldest surviving son." Viktor snorted. "You'd think Aron's father does sit on a throne, instead of being heir to a throne that hasn't existed since the Sons of Darkness swallowed Betavar. That's him over there," he said, pointing through the crowd.

Haefen stared in that direction, shifting until he saw a man with a blue-sleeved tunic matching Aron's. A young girl stood beside him, tugging on his hand.

"And lucky you. We heard today that Aron's also begun his last weeks of apprentice training. The two of you may end up approaching the Qodesh at the same time."

A dark-haired man stepped onto the stage, dressed all in black. When he held up his hands, the crowd quieted and found seats on the stone benches.

"That's Master Long," Viktor whispered. "He's visiting from Fusang."

Haefen leaned forward in his seat. He'd never seen anyone from Fusang before.

It turned out to be a combat demonstration. Master Long had the two groups line up facing one another along the front of the stage. First they fought with kicks and punches, like a dance. Not to hurt each other, but to knock each other off balance. Or even to wrestle their partner to the floor.

Then Master Long handed them wooden swords. Weapon whacked against weapon, almost too fast to follow, as the apprentices circled their partners, searching for openings in their guard. The swordplay was impressive. Haefen had fought with his fists and a staff, but never with a sword.

Aron's swordplay stood out from all the others. His partner was hard pressed to fight off his attacks, backing and turning as Aron advanced, but never taking the offensive himself. Haefen studied Aron's techniques, wondering how he'd fare using his staff to counter Aron's whirling sword. Not well. A staff was longer than a sword, and slower.

The crowd called out to their favorites, shouting and applauding when anyone scored a hit. The fighters would have bruises tomorrow. Haefen glanced over to where Aron's father sat. He was on the edge of his stone bench, leaning forward and shaking his fist, cheering Aron on.

Master Long called an end to the fighting before Aron's partner could fall off the back of the stage. The combatants bowed to their partners and stacked their swords at Master Long's feet. Then they headed back to where they'd started, reforming the two groups on either side of the stage.

Master Long thanked the crowd for coming, and bowed to the apprentices before stepping off the stage. The crowd surged to their feet, ready for their dinner.

Haefen stood and followed Viktor down the steps. His legs felt a bit wobbly. It'd been a long day. His head still ached, which was understandable. But his body ached too, as if he'd been in a fight of his own. And his stomach felt hollow.

Maybe he'd see Laurelin in the dining hall. He quickened his steps.

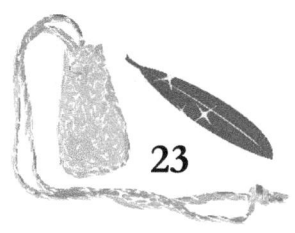

23

She'd had her fill of the tannery by the end of the day. Laurelin trudged back toward the dining hall with Brother Udi and some of his friends, grateful she'd get to eat somewhere that didn't stink. She'd only choked down a few bites of the picnic lunch Brother Udi had shared with her. Her arms ached from scraping hides, and she smelled like simmering goat brains.

She felt good about her day, even though tanning was worse than anything her dad had ever made her do. It was harder than yard work. And more disgusting than cleaning toilets. But she'd worked hard all day, and Brother Udi had been pleased with her.

"So, can I come again tomorrow?" she asked.

"If you can face another day breathing tannery fumes, I'd be glad of your help."

A mass of people surged out of the amphitheater and joined them on the path. Brother Udi tsked. "Forgot about the apprentice demonstration. You might have enjoyed it, Laurelin."

They stopped and waited for the crowd to thin. Some of the people were headed to the same dining hall they were, while others strolled west, back toward the tannery.

Laurelin spotted Haefen chatting with another apprentice, the two of them making their way toward the dining hall. "I'll see you tomorrow," she said, giving Brother Udi a quick wave.

She squeezed through the crowd, passing people right

and left, until she drew level with Haefen. "Hi," she said, trying to sound casual. She didn't want him to think she'd been chasing him down.

Haefen grinned. "Hello, Laurelin. You have an interesting aroma."

"Maybe because I've been working in a tannery all day. I'm going to work there tomorrow too."

"Laurelin, this is Viktor."

"Hey, Viktor. So you're going to enter the Qodesh too?"

Viktor chuckled. "Eventually, but not any time soon. I'll see you later, Haefen," he said. "I need to talk to Greger about tomorrow." He jogged ahead and tapped another apprentice on the shoulder.

"What do you bet that was an excuse to get away from my smell?"

Haefen laughed. "I'm glad of your smell, if it means I get you to myself." He paused. "There's something I wanted to talk to you about."

They'd reached the dining hall by now, and Laurelin waited in line behind Haefen until it was their turn to fill their plates. The food smelled amazing. She took a deep breath of her meat and gravy while they threaded their way to an empty table.

A ripple of conversation followed along behind them. Probably from people pointing out the new apprentice, and wondering who that girl was with him. Laurelin smiled, nodding to everyone who turned around to stare. No reason for them to think she was a shrew.

"So what did you want to talk about?" she asked, once they'd sat down. The dining hall was noisy tonight, and most of the tables were filled. A group of apprentices laughed and chatted on the opposite side of the hall, but Haefen had chosen a small table well away from them.

"I talked to Brother Efrat on Sunday, before Sabbath

service."

"Who's Brother Efrat again?"

"We saw him on our first night here. The brother who led the service?"

"Oh, right. Gandalf."

Haefen raised his eyebrows.

"Never mind. So you talked to him about the Qodesh? Your name and all that?"

Haefen glanced over at the other apprentices, and then stared at his plate. He stirred his food around but didn't eat. "Yes. He said it's best if I use my true name, my birth father's name, during my attempt to enter the Qodesh. And of course, I don't know it."

He twisted his ring and sighed. "There's a chance Brother Efrat can help me learn who my parents were. But if he can't, my journey was pointless."

He smiled at Laurelin. A sad smile, uneven and adorable. "I just wanted to let you know. Because if Brother Efrat can't help me find my father's name, I might start my journey home before the week is up. It's useless to stay if I can't enter the Qodesh. But then you might leave before me, if the Puerán help you return to the Shimmertree and your family. Have you asked someone about that?"

"Not yet." She was worried about getting home, but she didn't want to leave before Haefen did. "Let's eat before our food gets cold." Laurelin was starving, but she hadn't wanted to stuff her face while Haefen poured his heart out.

She took a bite of some kind of orange vegetable, steamed and dripping with butter. Who knew vegetables could taste so good? Even Benjamin would eat this. But she'd never get anything on Earth to taste this good unless she went grocery shopping on Piqqeah.

Haefen sighed and picked at his food. "I've wanted this since I was small."

Laurelin set down her fork. "Then don't give up. It's

less than a week now. If you give it your best shot, who knows what'll happen? I mean, Abba El wants you to do the Qodesh thing, right? So I'm sure he'll help if you just do the best you can."

Haefen smiled his sad smile. "All right, Laurelin, I'll trust in Abba El. Maybe I'm just tired. It was a long day."

"So tell me about the other apprentices," Laurelin said, nodding toward the large table where they sat.

Haefen gestured with his fork. "Do you see the one with the blue sleeve?"

"The one in the middle?"

"Yes. That's Aron Ben Fredrik."

Laurelin shrugged. "So?"

"Aron is the eldest son of the eldest son, all the way back to King Beraqel."

"Wait, I thought the uncle killed Beraqel when he took over the kingdom."

"Yes, but Queen Elin escaped here, to Mount Nevo, with the king's newborn son. She wore the king's own breast-plate concealed under her robe for the child's inheritance, hoping that someday the kingdom would be restored to the rightful heir."

"So that was Beraqel's only child?"

"The only one who lived. I was named after Beraqel's firstborn son, but the Sons of Darkness killed that child so he couldn't grow up and rally the people to avenge his father. I'm sure Queen Elin wouldn't have escaped death if the uncle had known she was with child. She fled Betavar before her pregnancy showed. They say she was spared because Javan desired her for himself."

"Okay, that's creepy." Laurelin wiped her mouth and picked up her empty plate. "Hey, Haefen, I'm gonna take a bath and get rid of this odor. Will I see you tomorrow?"

Haefen smiled. "I hope so. Thank you for your words, Laurelin. You've given me hope."

She dropped off her plate and headed for the door. She'd hated to leave Haefen sitting there alone, but she couldn't stand smelling like essence of goat any longer.

24

Aron escaped as soon as his plate was empty, leaving the other apprentices to finish their meal. It was easy to eat quickly when you didn't spend the entire mealtime laughing about nothing.

He glanced toward the table where Haefen sat, alone now. There'd been a few jokes about him at dinner. No jokes about the girl he'd been with, though. She was too pretty for that. She'd come with Haefen or something, which was odd. Maybe girls in his village had decided boys shouldn't have all the fun.

Aron snorted. Fun. Yes, that's what he'd gotten himself into. A whole lot of fun he had planned for the rest of the week, if today was anything to go by.

He gave his plate to the dishwashers and turned toward the door, picturing his father's face when even King Beraqel's ring didn't magically open the crystal chest for him. Aron would be standing there like an idiot, while his father raged at him in front of the other elders.

Lost in thought, Aron bumped into a novice. He hadn't noticed the group waiting in front of the door. Though something smelled foul and tainted. "Sorry."

She turned, and shrugged. "No problem."

It was the girl. Not a novice. Aron gaped. She was even prettier up close. Her dark hair framed her face and her blue eyes.

"You're Aron, right?"

"Er, yes." Must be the blue sleeve again. He'd had to

wear it to the demonstration, of course.

"Hi. I'm Laurelin."

"Nice to meet you. Have you come to be a novice?"

"Oh, no. Just visiting, you know." She shrugged again.

Her speech sounded strange, but her voice was pleasant.

Aron smiled. "Welcome to Mount Nevo." And he sounded like a fool, as tongue tied as if he'd never met a girl before.

"Sorry about the reek. I was helping out at the tannery today."

"The tannery, yes. I know that smell." Aron smiled. "I spent an unforgettable day with Brother Udi a year or so ago, stirring barrels of noxious liquid, and stewing brains over the fire."

Laurelin chuckled. "Sounds a bit like my day. Brother Udi makes for interesting company, though."

Aron smiled. "Does he still run his grimy fingers through his hair?"

"All the time! He doesn't even realize he's doing it."

Brother Efrat called out from behind them, "Brothers and sisters? I need your attention a moment."

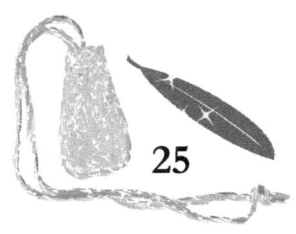

25

Laurelin turned. Brother Efrat stood by the dining hall door, his arms raised for silence.

When the hall quieted, Brother Efrat continued, "Brother Jeffree has left us to continue his eternal journey. We will all miss him, as his presence has been a blessing these last fifteen years. A Remembrance service will be held tomorrow evening."

A rumble of voices followed this announcement, but more subdued than before. Laurelin shrugged. The man had been on his last legs, so his death couldn't be too big of a surprise. And the doorway was finally clear.

She smiled at Aron. "See you around, I guess."

Outside the cloudy sky was almost as light as it'd been at noon. Crazy how you never saw the sun here, except for a brighter patch of cloud crossing the heavens. But the light of the Shechinah warmed her like the sun never had. Like every one of her cells could feel its warmth.

"Laurelin," a man called from behind her.

She turned. It was the Gandalf man. Brother Efrat.

"May I speak to you for a moment?"

"Sure." Haefen had probably said something about her needing help to get back to the Shimmertree.

Brother Efrat held out a small, leather-bound book, tied shut with a string. "Brother Jeffree asked me to give you this."

"What? Why?"

Brother Efrat smiled. "He wouldn't tell me why, but he

was adamant that you should have it."

Laurelin hesitated, but then took the book and untied the string. The cover was blank, but a title had been written on the first page in flowing gold script. "Past Glories." She frowned at Brother Efrat. "I don't understand."

"Brother Jeffree spent many years collecting stories about Betavar-that-was."

"Betavar?" Why would that doddering old man give her a book about Betavar?

"Brother Jeffree was engrossed with Betavar when he first came. He asked everyone to tell him any stories they knew, particularly about its last days. This book is a collection of all he learned, written in his own hand. To my knowledge, no one else has read it."

"Why not? I mean, after all that work?"

Brother Efrat shook his head. "I don't know, but you should consider it a sacred trust."

Laurelin shrugged. "Okay. Thank you." Weird. The man saw her once, then died the next day, leaving her his most treasured possession. "Uh, Brother Efrat? Haefen wanted me to ask you something, about how I can get home."

"Home?"

Laurelin glanced back toward the dining hall, but no one else was near enough to hear. "To my planet. The Shim-mertree guardian sent me to Piqqeah, to the stone circle where I met Haefen. But I guess it's a long walk to the Tree, and Haefen thought you guys could help. Maybe."

Brother Efrat smiled. "How blessed you are, to have seen such a glorious thing. Someday I'd like to visit the Tree myself." He stroked his beard. "I'll think on your dilemma. But if the Guardian sent you to meet Haefen, he must have a plan for you to return home."

Laurelin snorted. Too bad the Guardian hadn't mentioned this plan. "Sure. Thanks, for the book and every-thing."

Brother Efrat turned back toward the dining hall, and Laurelin flipped through Brother Jeffree's book on her way to the baths. Dark, neat handwriting filled the pages, interspersed with drawings and maps.

Laurelin shut the book and retied the string. The whole thing with Brother Jeffree was weird, weird, weird. She still thought the man had recognized her somehow in the House of Light, no matter what Olivia had said.

Laurelin washed her hair three times and scrubbed her skin raw before she was sure the smell of goat brains was gone. She pulled a clean dress over her head and paused to inhale the scent of fresh laundry. She couldn't remember anything smelling that wonderful before.

In the dormitory, the girls sat on their beds, studying and oblivious. Laurelin would fit right in. She tiptoed past them to her bed at the far end, and pulled back the covers. Leaning back against her pillow, cozy and comfortable, she stroked Jeffree's book. What was she getting into? But her curiosity won out over the weirdness.

She untied the string and opened the book to the title page again. "Past Glories." She stroked the gold letters with her finger, then turned the page. She sat up straighter when she saw the first line.

"Laurelin, you didn't tell me how soon you'd come. So I'll begin this now and hope it will be ready in time."

26

Haefen slept away his fatigue and woke with a bit of hope, built on Laurelin's words. Abba El desired him to enter the Qodesh. Haefen would be faithful, and wait on Abba El's help to find his father's name.

But his heart sank as he trudged westward. Yesterday had been a failure. And he couldn't bear to stare at the stone another day, hours on end, willing it to move.

He stepped inside the square room to find Brother Biorn meditating again. Haefen sat on the rug and closed his eyes, wishing his mind could focus like Brother Biorn had explained. He wriggled his tense shoulders. But his mind leapt in one direction, and then another.

He might as well beat his head against the wall of the Qodesh, instead of trying to walk through it. He'd get just as far either way. Was it this hard for everyone? Had his foster father felt discouraged too? Rohbert had never said much about his own experiences with the Puerán.

"Good morning, Haefen."

Haefen opened his eyes. "Good morning, Brother Biorn."

"Let's go for a walk."

"All right." Anything was better than meditating. Haefen followed him out of the room and into the light of the Shechinah.

Brother Biorn turned and shut the door behind them. Haefen waited, expecting him to follow the path around the nearest garden. Or maybe he'd walk toward the edge of the plateau. But Brother Biorn stood with his hand resting on the door handle, lost in thought. Maybe he'd forgotten something.

The minutes dragged on. Haefen thought about clearing his throat, or maybe asking Brother Biorn if everything were all right.

"There we go." Brother Biorn smiled. "Sorry that took a while. I'm not adept quite yet." He turned the handle and opened the door.

Instead of the square room they'd left, a stone-paved hallway had appeared out of nowhere. The hallway floor was two feet higher than the door's threshold, and sloped upward to their left.

Brother Biorn chuckled. "Could have done that better. Good thing Brother Efrat isn't here to see." He stepped up into the hallway, ducking so as not to hit his head on the lintel, and waited for Haefen to follow. "Come on then."

"Right." Haefen stopped gaping and stepped up behind him, leaving the door of the cottage open. He didn't know where they were, but if he shut the door, Brother Biorn might not be adept enough to get them back to the community.

The hallway was narrow and dim. They hiked single file up its gentle slope, walls of mortared stones on either side. The mortar left a chalky mark on Haefen's sleeve when he brushed against it.

They plodded along for several minutes, Brother Biorn's braid swinging back and forth with every step, until the hallway ended in a stone archway. Sunlight poured through the opening and bathed Haefen's face. He stepped through the arch and turned around, confused. The Shechinah was gone. They'd left the community.

"Welcome to Day's Eye." Brother Biorn started down a dirt path toward a squat stone box as large as the room they'd left.

Haefen followed. Brother Biorn wasn't explaining much

today. The clear sky was an intense shade of blue, and the sun was enormous. Fields of daisies stretched out to either side of them as far as Haefen could see. But the only path through the bobbing daisies led from the archway to the stone box.

Brother Biorn climbed down a square hatchway, set into the dirt at the end of the path. Haefen ducked his head and followed, descending a dozen stone steps to the chamber below. It was like a basement without a house.

Besides the open hatchway, the chamber's only illumination came from a small hole in the center of the ceiling. A large, rectangular cistern sat below the hole, hollowed out of a solid chunk of rock.

"Remove your outer clothing and climb in the cistern."

A long way to come for a bath. But Haefen took off his tunic, his shoes, and his pants. He hoisted himself up onto the edge of the cistern and poked a cautious toe into the water. It was as warm as bathwater. Reassured, he slid in and treaded water. The cistern was deeper than it appeared.

"Good. Now float on your back, Haefen."

Floating in the warm water, wiggling his hands and feet to find his balance, Haefen gazed at the ceiling above. It wasn't a hole in the ceiling, but a crystal, embedded in the stone like a tiny window.

Brother Biorn murmured something under his breath and snapped his fingers. The light from the crystal focused into a tight beam on the center of Haefen's bare chest. Brother Biorn snapped his fingers again and the light split in two, shining on Haefen's forehead now, as well.

"Close your eyes and relax, Haefen. Feel the two spots of warmth from the light radiating on your skin."

"I do."

"Focus on that warmth. Let it penetrate your flesh. Feel it illuminate your mind and pierce your heart. I want you to feel as though you're lit from within. Take as long as you need.

I'll wait outside."

Brother Biorn's footsteps retreated across the chamber and ascended the steps. Haefen opened his eyes and gazed at the ceiling. It was strange to see one spot of light descend in twin beams. But no stranger than the too-large sun shining on the daisy fields outside. He closed his eyes and focused on the warmth.

Time passed.

He stopped noticing the water lapping against his skin. The spot on his forehead burned and seared while his mind spiraled inward on a beam of light, turning and spinning, deeper and farther in. Immersed. Reaching. Then at last, centered.

The spot on his chest burned too, scorching hot, as if he were being branded. It was both painful and exhilarating. Tears trickled from the corners of his eyes, whether from pain or joy, he couldn't tell. He heard every drumbeat of his heart. His blood rushed through his veins to nourish his body, while the light streamed through his essence and fed his soul. Haefen felt larger inside than out. He nearly forgot to breathe.

He didn't know how long he'd been floating in the cistern. But when Haefen emerged into the sunlight, dripping and carrying his clothes, his hands had shriveled like prunes. His chest was unmarked. Outwardly, at least. He shivered as the water evaporated from his bare skin. The sun hadn't moved.

He didn't see Brother Biorn until he turned and found him perched on the roof, meditating. Haefen hoisted himself onto the roof as well. Then he stretched out full-length on the warm slab, pillowing his face on his bundle of clothes. The sun's warmth felt amazing.

Brother Biorn shook him out of a deep sleep. "Haefen, time for our midday meal."

How did he know? The sun still hadn't moved. Haefen pulled on his wrinkled clothes and followed Brother Biorn back to where the stone archway waited among the daisies. Haefen took a long look around, basking in the light of the alien sun, before stepping into the dim hallway beyond.

The afternoon found him sitting on Brother Biorn's rug struggling to light a candle. He'd lit a candle many times before of course, but never with his mind.

Brother Biorn had set the fat candle in the center of the rug when they returned from their midday meal. "You know the light of the Shechinah is the sign of his Presence?"

"Yes. It means the Puerán community is under Ben El's care."

"We enjoy a greater portion of His light, but the light of Ben El fills the immensity of space. It powers our sun and all the other suns that we see as stars in a night sky. His light is endless, infinite, and ever present. It illuminates our world, as well as our minds and hearts. Focus your thoughts and your desires on the light of Ben El, Haefen, and you will be able to light the candle." He leaned forward and blew softly on the candlewick until it flamed into life.

"Wait, how did you do that?" Haefen couldn't face another day like yesterday, straining and aching with desire, but still failing to do what came so easily to Brother Biorn.

"Breath is life, Haefen."

"Yes, but...."

Brother Biorn waved him to silence. "Just focus. It should come easier for you today than yesterday." He leaned forward and blew out the candle.

Haefen stared at the smoking wick. Focus. Right. He closed his eyes for a moment and breathed deeply, in and out, willing his tension to flow out and beyond him. Opening his eyes, he gazed at the candle. He let the sight of it fill his mind to the exclusion of all else. Let there be light. He leaned forward and blew.

The wick flickered at first, then flamed. Haefen gaped. "Did I do that? Maybe it hadn't gone completely out."

Brother Biorn smiled. "Do you doubt yourself? It's either impossible, or it's simple." He blew out the candle and licked his fingers before pinching the wick. "Is the candle completely out now, Haefen?"

Haefen pinched the wick with his own damp fingers. "Yes."

"So light it again."

He repeated his actions from before, like a ritual. Breathing out his tension, focusing on the candle, willing it to light, and giving it the breath of life. It flamed in an instant. Haefen shook his head with wonder.

"All things are possible to those who believe," Brother Biorn said softly. He moved the lit candle to one side and placed yesterday's stone between them. "Move the stone, Haefen."

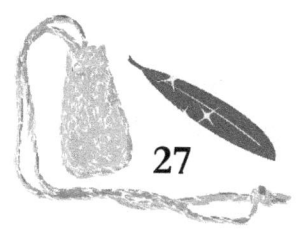

27

Everyone in the community had gathered to celebrate Brother Jeffree's life at his Remembrance service. The House of Light was bursting. And it was a celebration, not a time of mourning. Olivia had made that clear.

Laurelin sat with Olivia and the other novices. Everyone else sat in groups, too. Haefen was perched up on nosebleed row again. The apprentices filled the upper benches around the entire perimeter of the House.

The apprentice with the one blue sleeve, whatever his name was...Aron, sat on the opposite side of the building from Haefen. The novices near Laurelin kept glancing up at him, then whispering among themselves. Ogling him. Laurelin snorted. Haefen was more attractive, and probably nicer. Who else would have let her tag along on a five-day walk?

The younger children sat in tiers below the apprentices. The sisters sat in sections separate from the brothers. Novices filled several sections, though Laurelin didn't recognize all of them. There were plenty more dormitories than the one where she was staying.

The stone table on the floor below had been covered with a midnight blue cloth. Brother Jeffree lay on top of it, dressed in brilliant white robes that reminded Laurelin of the Shimmertree Guardian. Though Brother Jeffree didn't shimmer, of course. His arms lay by his sides, palm up, and a metal mask covered his face.

"What's with the mask?" she whispered to Olivia.

"You don't follow this custom?"

Laurelin shook her head.

Olivia leaned closer. "Brother Jeffree shed his cloak of mortality to continue his eternal journey. One day he'll receive an immortal body that shines like white fire, but until then the pewter mask represents his spirit shining unfettered by mortality."

"And that's why his clothes are white?"

"Yes, and the blue cloth represents the heavens where Abba El dwells."

It was strange seeing someone's dead body lying there without a casket. Would they give him one before they buried him? Did they bury people? She hadn't seen a graveyard anywhere.

During the Remembrance service, people took turns stepping down beside Brother Jeffree and sharing stories about him. Men and women, children and adults. Whoever wanted to. Many of them spoke about his exuberance and joy for life. Laurelin had a hard time imagining the old man she'd seen walking on his hands, but he'd been younger then, of course.

She puzzled over Brother Jeffree's book. How had he known she'd come to Mount Nevo? And why did he want her to have his book about Betavar?

Brother Efrat had been wrong. It wasn't a collection of stories. And it didn't say anything about Betavar's last days. It was an encyclopedia. Brother Jeffree had written about dozens of people from the time of King Beraqel, describing their appearance, their mannerisms, and their likes and dislikes.

He had one chapter all about the castle, with a map for each floor and all the rooms marked. Another page had a map of the city of Betavar. She found a map of the land of Betavar, too, showing a river running past the city's east side. An island lay downstream, with plains on the west, and mountains to the north. Why had Jeffree thought she'd care about all that stuff?

Brother Udi had helped Laurelin make a small leather pouch today, to hang around her neck. After she'd bathed, she'd tucked the Shimmertree leaf inside the pouch. She left her watch and Brother Jeffree's book in the dresser beside her bed. She understood the Puerán well enough now to know no one would go snooping in her things.

The leaf, though. She didn't want to leave that behind. She fingered the pouch now, feeling the living leaf pulsing inside of it, and wished it could help her understand more than just the language. Laurelin stared down at the body lying on the table. Who was Brother Jeffree? And how had he known her name?

28

The morning after the Remembrance Service, Haefen joined Brother Biorn on the rug and closed his eyes. Peace came swiftly when he opened his mind and heart to receive it. He breathed it in, allowing it to fill the still spot in the center of his soul.

"Welcome Haefen," Brother Biorn said. "I hope you slept well, because today will be tiring. Spiritual exertion has an energy cost just as physical exertion does."

"So that's why the last two days have been exhausting?"

Brother Biorn grinned. "Yes, and today will be even more so. Yesterday we talked about the endless and ever-present light of Ben El. You will never be anywhere his light can't reach. And just as it powers our sun, it can light your way through the darkness."

"Like Brother Sigurd's tunnel."

"Exactly. Did you ask him how his tunnel was lit after you passed through the Miphtan?"

"No, but I've been puzzling over it ever since, and that's the only thing that makes sense."

"What about this room? There are no windows, and the door is shut. Where is the light coming from?"

Haefen's jaw dropped as he gazed around the empty room. "I never thought about it. So we're sitting here in the light of Ben El?"

"We are. It's not something the community does as a general practice. But his light is more conducive to spiritual enlightenment, so apprentices learn faster than they do in the light of the Presence alone."

Brother Biorn raised his right hand and the light in the room dimmed, then faded away. Light seeped in under the door, but otherwise they sat in darkness.

"Haefen, today you'll learn how to see with his light, when all other light has failed you. You may choose to have others see his light, or not. But for now, it'll be easier if we both see it."

They sat in the dark for at least an hour before Haefen understood what Brother Biorn had taught him. But when he learned to wrap his mind around it, and taught his heart to understand, he could call the light at will. He could dismiss it in an instant. He could fill his hand with light, or the whole room. He could ask it to illuminate both their eyes, or his own alone.

It was a sacred thing he did, calling upon the light of Ben El, and his heart swelled with the joy of it. But Brother Biorn had been right. The spiritual exertion left him limp and shaking with fatigue.

"Time for a break, Haefen. Let's go for a walk and visit the flocks."

It was a pleasure to stroll in the light of the Shechinah. It renewed Haefen's spiritual reserves, and spoke peace to his soul. Brother Biorn led him along a path to the northwest corner of the plateau. They hopped the fence and sat in the grass to watch the sheep. One of the lambs wandered toward them, brushing against Brother Biorn's braid before nibbling Haefen's fingers.

"Ask the lamb where his mother is," Brother Biorn said.

Haefen's head jerked up and he stared at Brother Biorn. "Are you serious?"

"I am. I called the lamb over so you could talk to it."

"You want me to talk to the lamb."

"With your thoughts. You don't need to speak aloud. In

fact, it's better that you don't. Less diffuse."

Haefen eyed the lamb and worked to send it his thoughts, but the lamb only settled into the grass and went to sleep.

"Haefen, can Ben El speak to the lamb? Can he command the lamb, if he chooses?"

"Of course. He can command all things."

"The lamb doesn't know you. Doesn't recognize your voice. But it knows the voice of its creator. Speak with his voice, Haefen. Say what he would say. By his grace, you can be his mouthpiece."

It sounded so simple when Brother Biorn said things like that. But once again, Haefen struggled to wrap his heart around it. At least it was pleasant to sit in the grass, basking in the light of the Shechinah, while veins knotted in his forehead from the effort of trying to speak to the lamb.

The lamb's mother called it back before Haefen managed it, but Brother Biorn called out another. Speaking to the lamb was impossible, until it wasn't. Haefen would have shouted with joy when he succeeded, but he didn't want to alarm the flock.

The lamb sat up and looked him in the eye, startled at first. But it answered willingly enough. Haefen thanked the lamb and dismissed it. It wandered over to rejoin the flock, losing itself among the others.

On their way back to the cottage, they stopped by the kitchen and found two trays of food already prepared and waiting for them. They took them along to the cottage and settled themselves on the rug. Haefen inhaled appreciably. The food smelled divine, and he was starving after his exhausting morning.

But Brother Biorn cautioned him before he could take a bite. "I spoke to the sister in charge of the kitchen this morning, and asked her to poison our food."

Haefen's mouth opened, but no words came out. He

took a breath and tried again. "Why would you do such a thing?"

"The power of Ben El can neutralize the poison, so that it does you no harm."

Haefen swallowed. "And how will I know if I've succeeded?"

Brother Biorn chuckled. "You won't fall over dead."

Haefen lurched to his feet.

Brother Biorn raised a hand, still smiling. "I'm sorry, Haefen. Please be seated."

He waited until Haefen had settled back cross-legged on the rug.

"My levity was inappropriate, but you looked as though I meant to murder you. I assure you, I only want to protect you."

Protect him? By poisoning his food? "Do all apprentices go through this?"

"No, but Brother Efrat asked me to teach you all that I could in the time you have left. He didn't say why."

Haefen twisted the ring. It felt natural on his finger after all this time, as if it belonged. But it didn't. His stomach rumbled. Poisoned or not, the food smelled delicious. "Please teach me how to neutralize the poison."

Brother Biorn smiled. "How do you win a battle? If you're in charge and Asseldam attacks, what would you do?"

Haefen thought for a moment. "I'd need a strategy and resources. Trained men I could lead into battle."

"Good. Now what if the battle is inside your body?"

Haefen's mind was blank, and his food was growing cold. But he pictured a battleground inside his body with miniature brothers of the Puerán fighting off the Sons of Darkness. It made sense in a convoluted way. "The only difference is the size of the troops?"

Brother Biorn nodded. "Exactly."

29

A breeze wafted through the square, caressing Laurelin's damp hair. Brother Udi had sent her off early today, telling her to get some lunch and clean herself up. Today was market day, and he didn't want her to miss it.

A water clock stood in the center of the square, straddling a stream in a stone-lined bed. Olivia had pointed it out on their way to the House of Light, but they hadn't had time for her to explain how it worked. Laurelin strolled around the clock, stepping over the stream to see the back side of it. She didn't see any hands, and she couldn't read the markings. The leaf didn't help like it had with Jeffree's book.

It was easier to tell time by watching the brighter patch of cloud cross the sky. It was just past midday, so it should happen anytime now. Whatever it was. Brother Udi had refused to explain. But with a twinkle in his eye, he'd told her to wait by the water clock and watch Brother Efrat.

So here she was, but Brother Efrat was nowhere to be seen. Other people gathered in drips and drabs, carrying full baskets or empty cloth bags. Maybe they planned to set up a market in the square. But for now, they stood there in their cream-colored robes, chatting amongst themselves in groups of three or four. Waiting.

The people at the south end of the square parted to make way for two men carrying a big wooden frame, a rectangle taller than they were. They stood it up even with the water clock, on the east side of the square. The opening faced north and south.

Brother Efrat came hurrying along the path from the north, apologizing to the people he passed. "Sorry. Running late today, brothers and sisters."

But if he were, no one was upset. Come to think of it, Laurelin had never seen anyone upset here. She glanced up at the enormous cloud hovering protectively above them. That was probably why.

The rectangle had wobbled when the men first set it down, rocking on the cobblestones until one of them held it in place. But then the other man had knelt and laid his hand on the bottom piece, and the frame became rock solid. One of the men was leaning against it now, but he stepped aside at Brother Efrat's approach.

Brother Efrat gripped one of the uprights with his right hand, and the crowd hushed. Expectant. His lips moved, but whatever he said was too quiet for Laurelin to hear. He gazed through the empty rectangle. And then, it wasn't empty any more.

Laurelin jumped. Sunlight flooded through the rectangle, and she could see dirt instead of cobblestones. Then the Puerán lined up in front of it, blocking her view. They took turns stepping through the frame, thanking Brother Efrat before vanishing into the sunlight.

Laurelin sidled through the press of people and stepped over the stream to see the back side of the rectangle. She had a good view of the waiting Puerán through its opening. A woman was next in line, carrying an empty bag over her shoulder. She took a step and she was gone, like watching a magic show. A man came next, holding a basket of metal goods that clanked as he stepped into nothingness. Laurelin shivered. It was a bit creepy watching from this side.

"You're going to the market, Laurelin?"

Mr. Heir-to-the-throne Aron stood beside her, smiling as he watched the people vanish. No blue sleeve today. Maybe he was incognito.

"Can you explain how this door to nowhere works? The people all come back, right?"

He chuckled. "They're going to the market in Ruomu. But when they finish their shopping, or sell all their goods, they'll step right back through the doorway."

Ruomu. That's where Patrik was going with his soos. "What about the people already in Ruomu? Do they walk through the doorway and come here?"

Aron shook his head. "No. Only those who step through the doorway to Ruomu can step back through the doorway to Mount Nevo. The people of Ruomu can't even see the doorway."

"They just see people step out of thin air? That must freak them out."

Aron waved his hands in the air and made a funny face. "Just one of the many marvels of the Puerán."

Laurelin laughed. "So you're going shopping?"

"I am. Would you like to join me?"

The novices would all be jealous. But Haefen was busy, so she might as well. "Sure. I don't have any money though. You use money, right? I've never seen any here."

"We use money outside of the community, and I have plenty for both of us." He pulled a leather bag out of his pocket and jingled it while he grinned. "Enough to be decadent."

She laughed. "Oh, by all means. Let's go be decadent."

The line had dwindled while they'd been talking. Laurelin followed Aron around to the other side of the doorway and swallowed down her nervousness. She'd walked through solid rock. She could step through a magic doorway.

She expected it to feel strange. Intense. But it was like stepping through any other doorway. She'd boosted her courage for nothing.

They emerged just outside of town, on a dirt path leading into Ruomu. The sun beat down from a cloudless sky as they strolled past timber-framed houses coated with clay.

The roofs were thatched, and probably full of bugs. Laurelin stayed in the center of the path.

"So you didn't have to study today?"

Aron smiled. "I should be studying. But Master Long said the northmen might be at the market today, and I wanted to see the swords."

A castle came into view, perched on the hill above the town. Laurelin stared. She'd never seen a castle before. One of the walls had collapsed, and workmen swarmed around it.

They heard the market before they saw it. Peddlers shouted their wares to be heard above all the chatter. Dogs barked, running free between the stalls. It was like being at a Renaissance fair. Not that she'd ever been to one, but she'd seen one on television.

Many ethnic groups had gathered to the market, but their skin and hair color didn't set them apart as much as their clothing did. The Puerán were easy to spot in their cream-colored robes, but everyone else wore colorful clothes in all kinds of styles and fabrics.

Aron took her arm to keep them from being separated. "Welcome to the Ruomu market, Laurelin."

"What is all this stuff?" she asked, stepping closer to one of the stalls. Liquid sloshed in dark glass bottles when a man squeezed past them and bumped the stall. Baskets of polished stones jostled small jars of powders in all different colors.

The stall keeper smiled and nodded, his skin baked dark from the sun, and his hair a faded red. "Healing water and dragon blood, fresh from the desert," he said pointing to the bottles.

Laurelin frowned and turned to Aron. "Dragon blood?"

"Not from an animal," Aron said. "Khaznian dragon blood is made from tree sap. If anyone sold real dragon blood, it would be the people of Fusang, but they would think it a sacrilege."

"They have dragons?"

"You didn't know?"

A woman with black, tightly kinked hair manned the next stall. Her black skin shone in the sunlight, and she smiled to show even, white teeth. "A pendant for your girl?" she said to Aron. "A figurine, perhaps? I have all sorts of dragons." She stroked a carved, white dragon with one finger.

Laurelin stepped closer. "What are they made out of?"

"Sea teeth, milady. The pendants. The figurines are carved from soos bones, then soaked in tea to age them brown and show off the details. Three days to carve one this size. Or maybe you'd like a carved soos horn?"

Aron smiled. "Would you like a pendant, Laurelin? The locals do some splendid carvings."

Laurelin looked at the woman. "You're from Ruomu?"

She nodded. "That's right, milady. Born and bred."

Laurelin stroked one of the pendants. She wished she could see a real dragon. "The carvings are beautiful. Thanks, Aron," she said, "I'd love one."

30

Aron helped Laurelin string the dragon pendant onto the cord holding her leather pouch. She'd chosen well. The finely detailed carving needed only a breath to spring to life.

Laurelin fingered it and smiled. "Should we go find the swords?"

"Yes, I hope the northmen are here." Aron threaded through the jostling crowd with Laurelin close behind. The northmen would have come by sea, so their stall might be closer to the docks.

A grin split Aron's face when he spotted a man on the far side of the market with a long, braided beard and well-groomed blond hair. He wore a red, knee-length tunic over pants tucked into his boots, and an axe hung from his belt.

The northman's stall was heaped with swords of all lengths and weights, but the two vargeld swords lay separate from the rest. Aron stroked the smooth grip of the one on the left. The blade was half a bodylength long, the inlaid runes spelling out vargeld.

"May I try it?" he asked the northman.

The man smiled. He must know Aron couldn't afford to buy the sword. It's not like he had gold ingots weighing down his pockets. "Give it a swing, then."

Aron hefted it and took a step or two away from the stall, toward the open area near the docks. The balance was perfect, and the leather grip felt at home in his hands. He'd need to build up his muscles, though, if he wanted to wield it one handed and carry a shield.

Laurelin watched him cut and thrust. "What's so special about this sword?"

"It's forged from crucible steel, Laurelin. So it's stronger and harder to break, but thinner and more flexible. The edge will hold longer, and penetrate armor more easily."

"Armor? When are the Puerán ever going to be in a battle?"

Aron shrugged. "The outside world isn't safe from Asseldam's predations, and we have a duty to our fellowmen." He set the sword back with the others and stroked the runes along the blade. "Thank you," he said, nodding to the northman.

A tinker sidled up to Laurelin, his straw-colored hair greasy and lank. "It's you, isn't it? You changed your clothes. Almost didn't recognize you."

Laurelin grimaced and shrank back. "Hello, Patrik."

She knew the man? Aron stepped between them. "What do you want?"

"Don't mind me, brother. Not causing trouble. Just wondered if she wanted to trade her bracelet yet. Not wearing it today, though. Eh?"

"The lady has no wish to trade with you. You're Asseldaman, aren't you?"

The man took a step back. "Me? No, brother. Just a wandering tinker, not from anywhere in particular. Been through Asseldam, of course. Don't live there, though, you know."

Aron frowned. "So you have no news of Mahan, then?"

The tinker's eyes shifted away and then back. "Mahan, is it? I heard he's a priest, or some such."

Aron snorted. "Yes, something like that."

He guided Laurelin away from the tinker and back into the crowd. "Are you hungry?"

"Starved, though I don't know why. I ate a big lunch."

They followed their noses past silk and jade from Fusang, skinwriters from Ruomu, and knitted sweaters from the north. Laurelin wrinkled her nose at the dried fish, so Aron plucked some coins out of his pouch and bought them each a large, meat turnover dripping with juice. Then he led Laurelin out of the market and up toward the castle where they could enjoy the food in peace.

The hill was steep, and they saved their breath for the climb. But as they hiked past, dodging the loose stones hidden in the grass, Laurelin's head turned to watch the workmen repairing the castle wall. "I've never seen a castle before."

Aron smiled. "Then I'm glad you could. Let's sit over here," he said, guiding her to the western edge of the hill. "I love to watch the sea from up here."

They sat cross-legged near the edge of the cliff, while the waves crashed against the rocks below. A brisk wind blew from offshore, but the sun warmed them. And the meat turnovers were as good as he remembered. The flaky crust melted on his tongue, and the spices made his mouth water. Maybe the seller would tell him what spices she used so he could buy some for his mother.

Laurelin wiped the juice off her chin with the back of her hand. "This is the best pasty I've ever eaten. Thanks, Aron."

"You are most welcome. Thank you for your company."

"So what happened to the wall?" she asked, nodding toward the castle behind them.

Aron frowned. "The Sons of Darkness attacked Ruomu last fall. The sages of Ruomu beat them back. But if the battle had lasted any longer, the castle might have been demolished. The Sons have a new High Priest who is testing his strength."

"So that's why you might need a sword."

"Yes. The Sons of the Prince have always been our enemies, but lately they threaten the entire world. Enough of gloom, though." Aron stood and offered Laurelin his hand. "Ready to return to the mountain?"

Aron feasted his eyes on the sea one last time before leading Laurelin back down the hill, toward the doorway. But on their way past the market, Aron heard the cough of a tiger. He grinned. The doorway could wait. Laurelin had been impressed by the castle, but she'd love to see the tigers.

He found the tiger cage on the north end of the market, surrounded by children. Even Master Long was there with his son and daughter.

Laurelin squealed. "Tiger cubs?" She squeezed in with the children, kneeling beside the cage.

Aron bowed. "Master Long."

"Aron," Master Long said, returning his bow. "What did you think of the vargeld swords?"

Aron grinned. "Glorious. But I'll need to earn money if I ever want to own one. The elders wouldn't think it a valid reason to open the community's coffers. For now, could I increase the weight of my practice sword?"

Master Long hesitated. "For solo practices, perhaps. But not against an opponent. Come by the practice floor and we'll discuss it further." He tapped his children on their shoulders, drawing them away from the cage. "Baihu, Qing, time to return to your lessons."

Baihu grinned. "Aron! Father said if we stay, I can be an apprentice. Like you."

Aron's heart froze in his chest. "Master Long, are you thinking of returning to Fusang soon?" None of the brothers had as much combat skill as he did.

Master Long frowned. "We'd like to stay, but the news troubles me. The latest word is that Mahan has altered the citadel dungeon using your Puerán techniques." He glanced up to the castle on the hill. "Mahan's eyes are greedy, and his arm grows longer still. If it reaches Fusang, I must be there."

Aron was silent as he strolled with Laurelin back to the

doorway. Her eyes shone with delight as she chattered about the tiger cubs. But he couldn't join in her happiness.

Mahan had left the Puerán to join the Sons of the Prince, too power hungry to stay on Mount Nevo. And now he stood poised to swallow the world.

Aron shook his head. He didn't want to fight with Haefen over who got to wear the king's ring. That was seeking for power like Mahan had.

And he didn't want to stand beside Haefen in front of the Qodesh wall, waiting for the sun to rise, as if they were rivals. Entering the Qodesh should be a sacred experience, not a contest. His father would be angry, but that couldn't be helped.

Aron squared his shoulders. He'd tell him tonight.

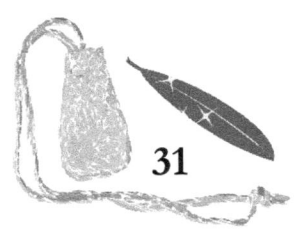

31

Laurelin ate breakfast with Haefen Thursday morning, then tagged along while he walked to the cottage to meet his tutor. She'd walked past that stone cottage every day on her way to and from the tannery. So when she'd finished up her day with Brother Udi, she dawdled on the path back to the dining hall and managed to time it just right.

"Laurelin," Haefen said, stepping out of the cottage and falling in beside her. He looked exhausted. Wilted even. He hadn't said much about what his tutor made him do, but it had to be even more strenuous than working in a tannery.

"Hey, Haefen. How was your day?" She held the rolled up piece of leather on her far side, waiting for the right moment to give it to him.

He showed her his hand, a wry grin on his face. "I guess you could say my day got a bit too warm."

Laurelin gaped. "What happened?" The palm of his hand was blistered and red.

"I did well in the morning, learning to put my hand in a flame without taking harm. But I was over confident in the afternoon while learning to emit energy from my palm." He shrugged. "My tutor makes everything look so easy."

Putting his hand in a flame? These people were crazy. "You need a bandage on that. It's gotta hurt something awful." Too bad she didn't have any painkillers to give him.

"Brother Biorn suggested I go to the house of healing. He said they're better at it than he is." He smiled. "Would you like to go with me? Or are you too hungry to wait?"

"Lead on, Macduff, to misquote Shakespeare."

Haefen raised his eyebrows.

Duh. He'd never heard of Shakespeare. "Sorry. I meant, I'd love to go with you."

"Thank you, Laurelin. I'd be glad of your company. I think we turn left after that big square building." He gestured further down the path, then gave her a closer look. "Is that a new pendant?"

Laurelin fingered her dragon pendant. She'd hidden it down the neckline of her dress over breakfast, but it had slipped out while she was working. "Remember I told you I went to the market yesterday? It's from Ruomu."

"The workmanship is excellent. But where did you find the money?"

Awkward. "Aron paid for it."

"Aron Ben Fredrik bought it for you?" Haefen frowned and gazed down at the cobblestone path.

"Well, he went to the market, too."

"I'd have thought he'd be too busy learning how to enter the Qodesh." Haefen studied his blistered palm. "Though it probably comes easier to him, since he's lived here all his life."

Laurelin sighed. She'd blown it. This was probably as good a time as any. "I made you something." She handed Haefen the piece of leather.

He smiled when he unrolled it. "This is the perfect size to replace the flap on my pack."

"That's what I thought. I made it myself, from beginning to end. Brother Udi said I'm his best apprentice." She snorted. "Of course, I'm his only apprentice."

"What do these markings mean?"

"I carved your name in English. What they speak on my world. I didn't know how to write it the Piqqeah way, but I thought you might like it."

Haefen traced the letters with his finger. "I do. Maybe I

could learn your language some day." He chuckled. "Then we could write each other secret messages."

Laurelin grinned. Haefen was talking like he'd see her again. Like this week wasn't the end. Maybe she hadn't blown it too badly.

The thought still made her smile the next day, while she helped Brother Udi tan more hides. Secret messages.

Laurelin hated scraping hides. Brother Udi had a backlog of stiff hides stacked and waiting to be tanned, and she had to scrape the bloody bits of rotting flesh off before he could soak them. When she was ready to gag, she'd go pump water from the stream to fill the soaking barrels. Brother Udi went through a lot of water.

Even though she spent most of the day grossed out, Laurelin enjoyed working in the tannery. Brother Udi made her happy just being around him, and he needed her help.

Friday afternoon, Brother Udi stepped out of his workshop and walked over to where Laurelin crouched. She was keeping a close watch on a hide she'd propped over the smoking fire. He picked up one of the hides she'd already smoked, and examined it, turning it over to see both sides.

Perspiration plastered her hair to the back of her neck. If Haefen were here, he could braid it for her again. Laurelin smiled. Just like when they'd braved the swamp. She probably looked as good now as she had then. Instead of green ointment, she had a streak of soot on her cheek where she'd wiped at an itch. And she stunk like goat brains. But the hides had turned a creamy brown from being smoked, and they were ready to be used.

Brother Udi set down the hide. "Very nice, Laurelin. I must be a good teacher."

She laughed. "You've been a great teacher."

"Just finish that one hide and we'll call it a day. Tonight is story night and you'll want to get cleaned up before dinner."

"Story night?"

"Oh yes, Laurelin." He crouched down beside her. "And we have some of the best storytellers among the Children of Light. I promise, you'll laugh and you'll cry." He grinned. "I'm excited."

"But you must have heard all their stories by now."

"Well, I must tell you that it's the newcomers who excite me." He waggled his eyebrows.

"Newcomers?" She swallowed.

"Yes, everyone new to the community will entertain us with a fresh story. That hide looks quite done. We can be off," he said, rising to his feet.

Laurelin jumped up. "Brother Udi, I can't stand in front of everyone and tell a story."

"You'll do great, Laurelin. You must know many excellent stories."

She frowned. "Not really.

And if she had to tell a story, she'd rather be home telling it to Benjamin. She missed his dirty face and his fierce hugs. She even missed her dad. But if she were home, she wouldn't be near Haefen.

32

The house of healing had done a wonderful job. Haefen fingered his unmarked palm as he approached the cottage. Today he'd focus on remaining humble and teachable. He grimaced. He didn't want another setback, especially if the teachings came so easily to everyone else. He thrust away the image of Laurelin wandering around the market with Aron, and stepped inside the stone cottage.

No matter how early Haefen arrived, Brother Biorn was always there before him. Haefen sat cross-legged on the rug and joined Brother Biorn in meditation, opening his heart to the peace of Ben El.

His peacefulness lasted until Brother Biorn asked him to try, once more, to shoot energy from his hand. Haefen could light a candle, or the room. He could even move the stone now. But he couldn't shoot a flame like Brother Biorn wanted.

Yesterday Brother Biorn had leaned a log against the far wall and repeatedly bathed it with fire to show Haefen how it was done. But Haefen's palm had sparked, not flamed. And instead of burning the log, he'd burned his hand.

Brother Biorn set the log between them on the rug. "I spoke to Brother Efrat last night about your difficulty with the flame. He suggested you try it without the ring."

Haefen bit his lip. "But I can't take off the ring. Brother Efrat must have told you."

Brother Biorn smiled. "You couldn't take it off on the Sabbath. Are you sure you can't take it off today? You can move the stone now, after all."

Haefen twisted the ring, trying to remember what Brother Efrat had done that day in his office. Haefen stroked it, and whispered a command in the name of Ben El. And the clear ring slid off his finger as if it had never been stuck. Haefen grinned and tucked it into his pocket.

"Now the log, Haefen. See if you can emit a gentle flame, to burn the log but not your hand."

But it was useless. Sparks flew like flint striking steel, but the energy he emitted had no flame. At least Haefen managed not to burn his palm again.

Brother Biorn shrugged. "No matter. Put on your ring, Haefen, and I'll explain how to fold the soil beneath your feet."

Haefen pictured a patch of dirt folding like a sheet of paper, and shook his head. "What does that mean?"

"Folding the soil is how the Puerán travel when they have need. It's how the Shimmertree Guardian sent your friend to the stone circle."

"You know of Laurelin's plight?"

Brother Biorn nodded. "Brother Efrat spoke of it to me in confidence."

"So, if the Puerán can fold the soil like the Guardian did for Laurelin, why don't they send Laurelin back to the Shimmertree?"

"We don't have the power to send another as the Guardian does, but only to fold the soil under our own feet, and only then in the service of Abba El. It's not meant for saving a walk to the dining hall."

"So that isn't what you did when we traveled to Day's Eye?"

Brother Biorn shook his head. "No. I created a temporary gateway. And before you ask, we can't create a gateway for Laurelin to travel back to the Shimmertree."

Haefen thought for a minute. "Could I fold the soil to

enter the Qodesh?"

"No. The Qodesh wall serves as a checkpoint, and can't be bypassed." Brother Biorn smiled. "Any more questions?"

"Not that I can think of right now."

"Don't worry if you don't grasp the principle at first, Haefen. Learning to fold the soil is difficult, and beyond the ability of most apprentices. I wouldn't have spoken of it, but when I told Brother Efrat of your progress, he suggested I explain it to you.

"You know that our planet, Piqqeah, has a spirit, as do all living things, though her spirit is not the same kind as ours. We are the spirit children of Abba El, while Piqqeah is his creation."

Haefen nodded.

"Folding the soil beneath your feet is a matter of joining your soul to hers, and then separating. You might think of it as entering her soul at your current location, and exiting at your desired location. That's not how it works, but it might help you picture it."

Haefen gaped at Brother Biorn. "You mean, I'm supposed to become part of the planet?"

"Temporarily."

Haefen's mind boggled, and he shook his head as if to clear it. "How do you practice something like that?"

"It'll be easier for you to feel connected to Piqqeah if we go outside."

Haefen spent the rest of the morning, and most of the afternoon, standing barefoot in the clearing east of the dining hall. It was the most pristine spot on the plateau. He and Laurelin had both stepped into this clearing from Brother Sigurd's long hallway, but Haefen saw no sign of the large doors.

Soaring beech trees with large trunks surrounded the clearing. Their spreading branches interlocked with their nearest neighbors, leaves rustling in a summer breeze. Dead leaves carpeted the ground over a layer of moss.

Haefen wiggled his toes in the moss. His back was toward the dining hall, but he could still smell the midday meal. Or maybe the scent of the evening meal was wafting around the clearing. He glanced over to where Brother Biorn sat leaning against one of the large trunks, his braid coiled beside him. He was either meditating or napping.

Despite all his effort, Haefen hadn't moved from this spot. At one point he'd felt a flicker of understanding about how to fold the soil, like he'd made a connection to Piqqeah. But the idea was as large as Piqqeah herself, and the thought had only glimmered before it evaporated. Haefen gave up and flopped down beside Brother Biorn.

Brother Biorn opened his eyes, then yawned and stretched. "I told you it was a difficult principle to grasp, Haefen. But don't give up. Keep practicing when you get home to your village. One day you'll realize it's either impossible, or it's simple. Just like the candle and the stone."

"And I don't need it to enter the Qodesh."

"Not at all. You're ready to make your attempt this Sabbath, as you'd planned. Brother Efrat will interview you tomorrow to assess your readiness, but I know he'll agree with me."

Haefen smiled. "Thank you for your help, Brother Biorn."

"You are most welcome, Haefen. And I'm looking forward to hearing a story from you tonight."

Haefen chuckled. "I know just the one I'd like to tell. Laurelin shared it with me on our journey here."

Brother Biorn left him then, and Haefen lay under the trees and gazed into the light of the Shechinah. Brother Biorn was confident he could walk through the wall of the Qodesh. But Brother Biorn wasn't aware Haefen didn't know his father's name.

Haefen grimaced and twisted the ring. So what if he

could speak to a lamb and light a room? He might have the skill to enter the Qodesh. But without his father's name, Haefen didn't have the permission.

He'd hoped Brother Efrat would have said something by now. Haefen had put off worrying, convincing himself that Brother Efrat would find the answer he'd been seeking. And maybe he would. Maybe Brother Efrat had been waiting to tell Haefen during his interview tomorrow.

Laurelin had told him to do his best and rely on Abba El. And Haefen had done all he could to prepare himself for that moment when he stood before the wall of the Qodesh.

He breathed away the knot in his stomach. Worrying wouldn't help. He'd hold onto the hope Laurelin had given him and enjoy himself at story night. And tomorrow he'd speak to Brother Efrat.

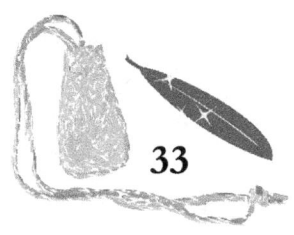

33

Laurelin sat amongst the rest of the community listening to a funny story. But while the storyteller flapped his arms like a giant raven greeting some star voyagers, Laurelin hugged her knees and racked her brain. She needed a story she could tell when it was her turn.

Haefen sat beside her, laughing so hard he had to hold his stomach. He leaned over and whispered, his breath warm on her ear, "Is it all right if I use your pig story, Laurelin?"

"Be my guest." Haefen looked so happy. His whole countenance radiated joy, even though she knew he was still worried about the Qodesh. If only she had her phone to take a picture of him like that, smiling at her with his deep blue eyes.

Laurelin dragged her eyes away from Haefen's face. There weren't many stories she remembered well enough to include all the details. Not without a book. She'd narrowed it down to either Little Red Riding Hood or The Little Red Hen. Weird how they both had Little Red in their titles. But the wolf had more drama than a bunch of lazy farm animals. Laurelin tried to relax. She'd picked a story. But she still had to stand up in front of everyone and tell it.

The raven story finished with a flourish, and the arm-flapping man squeezed back to his seat amongst much clapping and cries of, "Well told." Haefen jumped to his feet and made his way down the steps to the cleared space at the front of the amphitheater. Laurelin sat up.

Haefen smiled at the crowd. "My friends, I bring you a tragic story from a far away land. It teaches us to keep our noses to ourselves." He grinned. "And out of other people's chimneys. Once upon a time there were three little pigs."

During the story, Laurelin laughed and clapped her hands along with everyone else. Haefen turned out to be a great storyteller. He strode around the stage showing where each pig built his house, and made all kinds of building noises while he described their efforts. He gave each pig a different voice, and the wolf a gruffer, deeper voice. He had everyone in the crowd holding their breath when he described the wolf climbing down the chimney, his claws scrabbling on the bricks. They cheered when the wolf fell in the pot of boiling water, and applauded when Haefen finished.

Haefen waved his thanks and returned to his spot by Laurelin. But instead of sitting down, he held out his hand. "Come, Laurelin. You tell wonderful stories."

She let Haefen help her up, but her knees trembled as she edged her way along their row and down the steps. When Laurelin turned to face the crowd, she spotted Brother Udi sitting beside his wife and some of his friends. He smiled, and nodded to encourage her. She cleared her throat and began to speak.

"Once upon a time, in a village far, far away, there lived a little girl. Her mother loved her very much, and her grandmother loved her even more. Her grandmother made her a beautiful red cloak, with a hood for when it was cold. The little girl loved the cloak so much, she wore it all the time. So the villagers called her Little Red Riding Hood."

Little Red's mother told her not to talk to strangers, but the wolf was too fascinating to ignore. Laurelin described the wolf's deep voice, his big eyes, and his pointy teeth. She left out his big hands. Wolves had paws, not hands. Not that wolves went around talking to people, but still.

She used the ending where the hunter cut open the sleeping wolf and filled its body with stones. Benjamin always complained about that part. "No way he'd sleep through that,

Laurelin. And how did he swallow the people whole? He's not a snake."

Laurelin's knees trembled until she sat back down. She could have told the story with more flair, but she'd been too flustered with all those watching eyes. They'd all clapped, though. And for as much as they liked stories, it would've been hard to go wrong telling them one they'd never heard.

Haefen leaned closer and smiled. "Well told, Laurelin."

Many people came up afterward to thank Haefen for his story about the pig brothers, and to tell Laurelin how much they enjoyed hearing about Miss Hood. Brother Udi said, "See, I had good reason to be excited. And next week you can share more of Miss Hood's adventures."

Laurelin just smiled. She'd be gone by next week. But she wondered if Little Red Riding Hood did have more adventures, or if she'd learned her lesson about talking to strangers.

34

Haefen hadn't realized they'd have a dance at the end of story night. He loved dancing. He grinned. He could teach Laurelin how to dance the polka, unless she had the same kind of dance on her world. She looked so much happier now that the story part of the evening had ended. More relaxed.

The crowd cleared a dance area, while the musicians gathered at one end of the stage. They tuned their instruments, tightening strings and practicing beats, creating a cacophony that echoed around the amphitheater.

Laurelin gestured toward the musicians. "So, what are all those instruments? I mean, I recognize the xylophone, but what's that horn thing?"

"That a ram's horn. The man makes different sounds by tightening his cheeks, or moving his tongue. Even by the way he shapes his lips."

"So, like a trumpet. And what are those string things? Harps?"

"Those are zithers. The players use a piece of sea turtle shell to pluck the silk strings."

"They have an awful lot of strings."

"Yes, eighteen or so, I think."

A group of apprentices wandered over while they waited for the dancing to begin. Haefen recognized them from the dining hall. Viktor had called them Aron's flatterers, but

Aron was nowhere to be seen. Thankfully.

"We enjoyed your stories," one of them said, raising his voice above the noise of the musicians.

The others nodded and chimed in their agreement.

"My name is Yakob," the first boy continued. He shrugged. "We've never met, but everyone knows who you are, of course. You must be tired, Haefen. We're all dreading that grueling last week before we make our own attempts on the Qodesh. Maybe you could walk with us for a bit, away from the noise, and share any suggestions you have. We'd like to hear an outsider's perspective."

Haefen glanced at Laurelin. He didn't want to miss any of the dancing. But it wouldn't hurt to talk with them a few minutes, and he'd like to meet more of the apprentices.

Laurelin smiled and waved him away. "Go ahead, I'm fine. I wanted to ask Olivia something, anyway."

So he followed the apprentices past Viktor and Greger, who were eyeing a group of novices, and along a back way out of the amphitheater. Haefen hadn't noticed the dirt path before this. It wound westward through a thick grove of spruce trees that crowded against the path, leaving it shadowy and dark.

But the path meandered back into the light before too long, hugging the southern edge of the plateau. The boys had been joking and fooling around until then, with Haefen faking a smile and trying to join in. But when the trees ended, the joking ended, too.

"How about we sit here and show Haefen the view while he tells us about his week?" Yakob sat on the edge of the path, his feet dangling over the cliff, and motioned Haefen to sit beside him.

The southern slope of Mount Nevo spread out below them. But the light of the Shechinah didn't extend as far as that, and the sun had set hours ago. Haefen couldn't see much besides hummocks in the darkness that might have been trees.

No stars were visible. They couldn't compete with the light of the Shechinah.

A jumble of rocks littered the base of the cliff eight or ten bodylengths below. And even while he watched, more rock crumbled off and joined the heap. Haefen tried to scoot back from the edge, but Yakob dropped his arm over Haefen's shoulder and held him where he was. The other boys crowded in behind and around them, trapping Haefen in place.

Yakob squeezed his shoulder. "That's an interesting ring you have on your finger. Don't think I've ever seen the like."

Haefen twisted the ring. Brother Efrat hadn't said to keep it secret, but Haefen wouldn't be badgered into talking about it. He swallowed, his mouth dry. "I haven't seen one like it either."

"Did your father give it to you? But you don't have a father, do you? At least, not a legitimate one."

The other boys snickered. "Whore's son," they whispered, chanting in unison. "Whore's son. Whore's son."

Haefen's jaw tightened. How could Puerán boys be so hateful when they'd been raised under the light of the Shechinah? They sounded almost gleeful. As if it were a jest to accuse him of being a bastard. No one in Phonteh would ever have been so offensive.

Haefen squirmed, struggling to break free. But the boys pressed in harder, scooting him closer to the cliff's edge. "I'll thank you not to malign my mother," he said, his face flushed. "And neither the ring nor my heritage are any concern of yours."

Yakob nodded. "You're right. How your mother spent her time doesn't concern us. But the ring is our concern, Haefen, son of no one."

Haefen gritted his teeth, but kept silent.

"You see, Brother Fredrik happened to mention that you, a nameless bastard, stole this ring from under the altar at the Domarring. Maybe you thought you could use it to trick your way into the Qodesh."

Haefen struggled once more to get up, but only managed to break off a few more rock fragments. "I'm not a bastard, and I've never stolen anything in my life."

"Really?" Yakob chuckled. "What do you call it, then? Looting?"

The others boys laughed, slapping Haefen on the back.

Haefen fought to regain his composure. "Let me go."

"Hand over the ring and you're welcome to go." Yakob nodded his head to the clump of boys behind them. "We've had enough chat."

One of them grabbed the back of Haefen's tunic and dragged him to his feet. Haefen twisted to break free, but by then he was surrounded. The boys smirked while he shifted, searching for a gap.

When Yakob stepped toward him, Haefen dove between two of the other boys. But they piled on top of him and forced him to the ground, grinding his cheek into the dirt while one boy sat on his back. Another boy sat on his legs, while others grabbed his arms, immobilizing him.

Yakob grabbed Haefen's right hand, bending back the finger to yank on the ring. "This belongs to Aron," he said, his breath hot in Haefen's ear.

Haefen gritted his teeth against the pain. Yakob would be annoyed when he realized the ring wouldn't fit over Haefen's knuckle.

"What's all this?" a man's voice called.

The heap of boys dissolved. Haefen lay still, his hand throbbing.

"We were just wrestling," Yakob said.

"Next time save it for the combat school."

Haefen pushed himself to his feet and stumbled past the boys filling the path. Two brothers stepped aside to let Haefen by.

When he reached the shelter of the trees, Haefen jogged

down the path back toward the amphitheater, holding his right hand in his left. If the two brothers hadn't come along, Yakob might have broken Haefen's finger trying to remove the ring. It felt sprained as it was, his knuckle already swelling.

The path turned toward the amphitheater, and he could hear the music. The dance had started.

Haefen emerged from the trees, and waited for his breathing to slow while he scanned the crowd. Laurelin had said she wanted to talk to a girl named Olivia, so she was probably watching with a group of novices.

But, no. Laurelin was dancing.

Haefen's breath caught in his throat while he watched her swirl past. Aron's arm guided her in the steps as they circled the amphitheater in line with the other dancers. She was laughing, as joyful as he'd ever seen her. But of course Laurelin was happy. She was dancing with Aron.

Haefen turned and stumbled out of the amphitheater. He was halfway to the dormitory before he could thrust away the image of Laurelin dancing in Aron's arms.

He brushed the dirt off his face with one sleeve and examined his throbbing finger. It was puffy and red, twice its normal size, though the ring had enlarged to accommodate the swelling.

Yakob's comments about his mother hurt more than Haefen's finger. If they were true, if his mother had.... Haefen choked back a sob. No. He wouldn't believe that of his mother.

But what if the ring weren't the circle in a circle mentioned in the note? Haefen shook his head. Then he was nameless.

His stomach knotted. His baby blanket was probably a hand-me-down, so his name wasn't even Haefen. He didn't know his own name.

Nameless.

Brother Efrat would be sure to tell him more about the

ring during his interview on the morrow. He had to. Otherwise Haefen would pack his bag and go home. He couldn't stand in front of the wall of the Qodesh, knowing he was nameless. That he would fail in spite of all he'd learned.

35

The music sounded amazing, better than Aron had ever heard it. Brother Waldron had finally found something the Taph wanted, so they'd traded him a set of their reed pipes. Brother Waldron refused to tell anyone what he'd traded to the Taph, but that didn't keep people from guessing.

Once he had the pipes, Brother Waldron hid out on the mountainside for weeks, practicing where no one could hear. Tonight was his first public performance, and the reed pipes blended well with the rest of the ensemble.

Aron had danced the first polka with his little sister, Qanaah. But after that, he'd made a beeline for Laurelin. He'd been watching her all through story night, while she sat there next to Haefen. Her story had been delightful. New, and different. And Haefen had left after story night, leaving Laurelin alone.

Laurelin was a joy to dance with. She'd had trouble at first while she learned the footing, but now she turned in his arms with ease, taking his hand on cue, and twirling around the amphitheater as if she'd been doing it all her life.

And her smile. It was irresistible.

They were nearing the end of their second dance when Aron saw Haefen stumble past and out of the amphitheater. He looked worn and lonely. Burdened even.

Fredrik had been angrier than Aron expected when he'd told his father he would not be rushed to the Qodesh. But Aron didn't regret it. Especially with Haefen looking so weary.

He bowed to Laurelin at the end of the dance. "Thank

you, milady."

She laughed, and fingered her dragon pendant. "Thanks for teaching me. And sorry about all the times I stepped on you."

He grinned. "Quite all right. It keeps me in my place when someone steps on me now and then."

He left Laurelin near a group of novices, and scanned the crowd for Olivia. His mother would be sure to ask if he'd danced with her, and one dance was a small price to pay to keep his mother happy. Aron didn't need more than one angry parent at a time.

Besides, Olivia was good-natured and pleasing to the eye. And she would have been just as friendly even if he weren't the heir. Aron had had more than enough of blue-sleeve friends.

36

Haefen woke early. Though, the light of the Shechinah made it hard to judge how early. He lay in bed staring at the ceiling while he twirled the ring around his swollen finger. He'd had the dream again. The one where Brother Efrat shouted, "You shall remain nameless!"

And he was nameless, whore's son or not.

Brother Efrat had said the ring was an answer to his prayer. The circle in a circle. But wearing a ring didn't tell Haefen his father's name. And after last night, he craved to know it more than ever.

Last night.

Haefen pushed away the image of Laurelin dancing with Aron. It was just a dance. If he had stayed there, instead of stomping off like a dismayed suitor, Laurelin would have danced with him as well. Haefen had been so busy learning this week that he'd hardly seen her. And now, like a fool, he had missed his chance to dance with her. She'd return to her planet, and he would never get another chance.

The other apprentices still slept, but Haefen was too restless to try. Time was running out. Not just with Laurelin, but with his chance to enter the Qodesh. What if he couldn't, and his journey had been in vain?

Haefen slipped out of bed and dressed. Stepping softly, he left the dormitory and strode toward the center of the community. The ground was wet, and the air had a morning chill. Haefen followed the stone-lined waterway that bisected the community until he saw a bushy wall on the western side of the path. An opening had been cut into the greenery. The entrance to the labyrinth.

Haefen stood in the opening, staring at the hedged path beyond it. He'd heard so many stories about the labyrinth, told on starlit nights around Phonteh's central fire pit. It wouldn't be easy to walk the path, but it might help him learn his father's name.

He stepped forward. The path ran straight west at first, between the two walls of foliage. So far it was a path like any other. The tension left Haefen's shoulders and he relaxed. The stories had been exaggerations then, embellished for the village's entertainment.

But the path turned left and spiraled to the right. Time slowed. Each footstep took longer than the one before. The effort to press forward became enormous.

Haefen's mind spun forward and backward. One moment he struggled to take a step along the path of the labyrinth. The next, he knelt at an altar, twelve years old, pledging his service to Abba El. The next step found him straining to hold up the Domarring's altar stone while he reached for the ring.

Another step on the labyrinth path and Haefen stood all in white, waist-deep in the ocean. Rohbert guided him downward and immersed him in the water, then lifted him out. Reborn.

Haefen no longer knew if he stepped forward or stood still. The visions flashed by so quickly now, one after the other. He was gathering eggs. Step. He was fishing with his brother, Daniel. Step. He was climbing the eastern face of Mount Nevo with Laurelin. And still the vast effort to take a step, as the spiraling path unwound before him.

He was a baby, gazing up into his mother's eyes. His mother's eyes, not his foster mother's. Haefen fell to his knees, willing the vision to continue. Tears streamed down his cheeks.

She was so beautiful. Her light brown hair hung in a braid over one shoulder as she cradled him in her arms. She swayed as she sang him a lullaby. Rute had sung the same song to his foster brother and sisters. Tears welled up in his mother's eyes while she rocked him back and forth.

Haefen wondered how he knew this was his mother. But he knew it with such surety that he shrugged away the thought. The vision was a gift of Abba El.

The baby's eyes, Haefen's eyes, shut, and his mother lifted him to her shoulder and held him close. His head snuggled into her neck as she hummed the rest of the song. The tears rolled down her cheeks now, and dripped onto the baby's blanket. The carefully stitched letters spelled out his name. Haefen. He no longer doubted the name was his. A ring on her finger matched the ring on his own, a gold spiral embedded in clear metal.

And then the vision had gone, and Haefen knelt alone on the path between the bushy green walls. His whole life had changed in an instant. He wasn't nameless. He was Haefen. And his mother had loved him.

He bowed his head and sobbed. "Thank you," he whispered to Abba El. "Thank you."

After a time, he wiped his face on his sleeve and staggered to his feet. This spot was sacred, and he wished he could mark it in some way. But it looked the same as any other bit of the labyrinth. Green ahead, green behind, and green on either side.

Haefen leaned forward and took a step, and then another, following the curving path once more. He swam out to the nearest rocky island for the first time, his arms flailing. Rohbert swam beside him with confident, easy strokes. Step. He sat cross-legged in a circle with the other boys, memorizing the words he'd say in front of the Miphtan's soaring stone wall. Step.

A man trudged along, leading a soos through a grassy valley. A baby strapped to the soos' back murmured contentedly as the beast plodded along. A baby wrapped in Haefen's blanket. Could his father be leading the soos? The man glanced back at the baby and Haefen saw his face. An older man.

With his next step, Haefen helped Daniel gather the eggs. Another step and he braided Maerta's hair while she struggled to run out the door after Daniel. Haefen cringed when his vision self lost his temper, dragging Maerta back by her hair. She cried, her face red and streaked with tears. And he ignored it, wanting only to finish braiding her hair.

The visions became harder to bear. Haefen saw himself, time after time, doing things that shamed him. Things he'd forgotten. Though seeing them now brought them rushing back. He thought he'd been such a good older brother. Such a model son. Such a hard worker. Such a devout worshiper of Abba El. But now he saw all the times he'd been none of those things.

Each step became a battle to go on. A struggle within himself to take yet one more step. His legs trembled with fatigue, and he longed to end the shame and the torment. But he couldn't cut the path short.

The path spiraled tighter, step after step, until Haefen stumbled into the center of the labyrinth and the visions mercifully ended. An altar stood in the green-walled circle.

Haefen dropped to his knees beside it and sobbed out his anguish. Never had he felt such regret, such remorse, as he did now. Seeing himself as Abba El saw him had needed all his courage. He'd seen more good moments than regrettable ones in the labyrinth, but his regret weighed heavy on his shoulders.

He cried until he'd cried himself out. Like a small child. And then he prayed from the depths of his soul, begging Abba El's forgiveness for all the weak, petty, angry moments. He prayed until his knees ached. Until peace washed over him in a great calm.

Haefen shifted to sit cross-legged. He leaned back against the stones of the altar, drained of sorrow and filled with joy. After a moment, he wiped his face with the front of his tunic. The sleeves were too small. He chuckled. He must look a mess. And he had half the labyrinth still to walk. The inward spiral had been an inward journey. But the stories all said the outward spiral was something else entirely.

Haefen gathered his courage and faced the path. He took one hesitant step, and then another. It spiraled to the left now. Tightly at first, then unwinding toward the labyrinth's exit. His steps weren't the strained labor of his inward journey. Instead, his tired legs glided along the path.

He saw the yellow spiral he'd drawn in miriel powder on the altar in the Domarring. Another step, and he saw the miriel spirals Rohbert traced on the chests of his newborn children when he gave them their names. Daniel, Kerstin, and little Maerta. Step. He saw the spirals in shells he'd found along Phonteh's shore. Step. Then the circling whirlpool on the largest island, when the tide flowed out through the rock.

A few more steps. Stars spiraled above him. Step. And time spiraled through the seasons as year piled on year. Step. His childhood spun past. Step.

His experiences accumulated in the spiraling pattern of his life like a mountain path circling upward. As it led him higher, it expanded his view of the world beyond.

Step. He saw himself on the spiraling path between the living walls of the labyrinth, but from somewhere above himself, like a bird. From this height the labyrinth had the shape of a bushy green tree, with the entrance path as the trunk.

Another step. His view spiraled up and away until Haefen saw the whole continent below him, like a living map. Step. Villages were born, and sometimes disappeared. Centuries flashed by. Step. Phonteh lay on the western edge, Ruomu to the north. Other villages lay scattered like grain in the chicken yard. Mount Nevo stood in majestic splendor. Eastward from Mount Nevo lay the dark smudge of Asseldam, and more villages dotted the land in that direction.

The Shimmertree glowed in the center of the continent, there in its sheltered valley between the white-capped mountains. North of the Tree, the Khaznian ruins crumbled in the desert. That vast, arid region gave way to forested hills. And a city. Such a city. Fusang took Haefen's breath away.

Step. The continent receded as Haefen soared higher. Oceans appeared. Higher. More continents. Higher. The planet itself, spinning beneath his gaze. Piqqeah. It was so beautiful, so pure, spinning away from him in a majestic dance through the solar system. Higher. And the sun took its planets dancing through the galaxy, as the galaxy spiraled through the universe. Haefen's heart ached with the glory of it. The endless creations of Abba El moved in an exalted dance through the corridors of time.

Another step and Haefen's view returned to reality. To the green walls of the labyrinth, and the spiraling path beneath his feet. He stopped for a minute, dizzy, and marveling at the world he lived on. Piqqeah, hurtling through the universe while he clung to its surface. He squatted and rested his hand on the warm dirt of the path. He felt connected to Piqqeah now. Like a member of the same family.

Just ahead, a white statue stood embedded head-high in the foliage to the right of the path. Haefen stepped closer. The statue of a bird gazed at him, wide-eyed and watchful. And beyond the bird, an archway. The exit. He had made it.

A bench stood nearby, facing the spiraling path to the Qodesh. Haefen collapsed onto it with a thankful sigh. His legs ached as though he'd run for hours.

Was he late for breakfast? Maybe he should have told someone where he'd gone, but he hadn't thought walking the labyrinth would take so long.

He still didn't know the name of his father, but his mother had named him Haefen. His mother. He closed his eyes and pictured her face. Rute and Rohbert loved him, and his mother had loved him too.

"Haefen, I'm glad to find you here." Brother Efrat settled himself onto the bench beside him.

Haefen smiled. "I awoke early and decided to take your advice to walk the labyrinth."

"You look more peaceful than I've seen you."

"Yes. I feel more peaceful."

They sat in silence, gazing at the path to the Qodesh. He had the rest of the day. His last day of preparation. Then Haefen would walk that path and enter the Qodesh. One way or another. With his father's name or not.

Anything seemed possible at that moment.

Brother Efrat patted Haefen's shoulder and rose to his feet. "Are you ready for breakfast after all that?"

Haefen's stomach rumbled. "Definitely. But I'll grab a fresh tunic on my way to the dining hall." He grinned. "This one's a little worse for wear."

Brother Efrat chuckled. "Clean yourself up and get something to eat. Then come by my office. We have much to talk about."

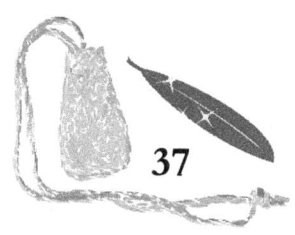

37

Olivia sat on the end of Laurelin's bed. "Good morning."

"Morning. Fun dance last night." Laurelin stretched.

Olivia chuckled. "Apparently you and I were the only ones to dance with Aron, besides his little sister. The other novices are annoyed, so watch your back."

Laurelin grinned. "I will. So, you guys are off today?"

"Yes, we spend Saturday with our families. I wondered if you'd like to join me and my family for the day."

Olivia was sweet. Too bad she didn't live in Pleasant Knoll. "Thanks, but I need to study a book Brother Jeffree gave me."

"That sounds like an interesting day, Laurelin. I wish you joy in it."

"Thanks Olivia. I hope you have a good day too."

She handed Laurelin a scrap of paper. "If you change your mind, I've drawn a map for you to find your way to our home."

When Olivia had gone, Laurelin slid Brother Jeffree's book out of her dresser drawer. She stroked the cover. Might as well bring it along to the dining hall.

She didn't see Haefen at breakfast. He'd probably eaten early and dashed off to do apprentice stuff. Tomorrow was his big day. Weird how he hadn't come back to the dance, but maybe the other apprentices had been helping him get ready. Hopefully he'd figured out his father's name by now.

Laurelin took her dirty plate to the kitchen and

wandered out into the clearing behind the dining hall. The leaves whispered in the breeze as the trees reached toward the light of the Shechinah. The perfect place to read.

She plopped down under one of the immense trees and stared at the cover of Jeffree's book. Hopefully he'd written about how he knew her.

Maybe it shouldn't bother her that Jeffree had recognized her. It would be creepy on Earth, but Laurelin wasn't on Earth. She'd traveled to another planet by Tree, sent by an angel. Weird things weren't as weird after all that.

But that start of recognition when Jeffree saw her in the House of Light. The way his eyes lit up, as if she'd been great friends with the old man in some alternate universe. And he remembered while she didn't. That was creepy.

Laurelin didn't know what would happen tomorrow. Maybe the Shimmertree Guardian would whisk her back to his hill as soon as Haefen entered the Qodesh. Or maybe the Puerán wouldn't let her take Jeffree's book out of the community, when she and Haefen trekked back to Phonteh. She needed to read the book today, in case she didn't get another chance. But still.

She stroked her dragon pendant and clutched the small leather pouch hanging beside it. The living, throbbing leaf comforted her. She leaned back against the broad trunk behind her and opened the book. "Laurelin, you didn't tell me how soon you would come...."

No use puzzling about that bit again. She flipped to the descriptions of the people. She could memorize their names and something about them. There were King Hoozeh and Queen Sheshna, Beraqel's parents. Javan was the name of King Hoozeh's brother. He must have been the wicked uncle who killed King Beraqel.

She flipped to the chapter on the castle and studied the drawings of each floor. She found the main entrance and traced her way through the castle, room by room, through corridors, and up stairways.

Laurelin found a bedroom labeled "King Hoozeh and Queen Sheshna," and another for Beraqel. One of the towers had a room labeled "Beraqel's tutor," but it didn't have the tutor's name. Laurelin flipped back to the people pages, but Beraqel's tutor wasn't listed. Brother Jeffree must not have learned anything about him.

Laurelin studied the map of the land of Betavar. From what Haefen had said, Mount Nevo lay almost straight west of the city, but the map didn't cover that much territory. It did show a whole chain of mountains north of Betavar, kind of in a horseshoe shape.

Something was written inside the horseshoe, in tiny letters. She peered at the minuscule writing. "First Garden," it said. That must be where the Shimmertree grew, surrounded by the snow-capped mountains.

Laurelin had studied most of Brother Jeffree's book by lunchtime. She rubbed her eyes and leaned back against the tree. Jeffree hadn't written anything about how he knew her, or why he thought she'd like a book about ancient Betavar. None of it made any more sense than it had before, but she'd read it. Done her duty, or whatever.

Saturday. Her dad would be home from work today. He and Benjamin were probably playing video games, or racing their remote-controlled cars, or making cookies. Laurelin smiled. Benjamin would be coated in flour, and the kitchen would be a mess. Dishes overflowing in the sink, the floor sticky.

Her eyes welled up and one tear trickled down her cheek. She'd been gone almost two weeks. They weren't making cookies. They were sending out search parties to hunt for her mangled body. Her dad would be worried sick, and Benjamin probably cried himself to sleep every night. What was she doing here, on another planet? The whole thing was crazy.

Could she trust the Guardian? He'd told her not to worry, back when she'd been sitting on his green hill. She gripped the leather pouch and felt the leaf pulsing inside it. She had to trust him. It would all work out, somehow. And after tomorrow, she and Haefen could leave the Puerán and hike back to Phonteh. Long days alone with Haefen. Laurelin smiled, and wiped her face on her sleeve.

38

Haefen walked away from the labyrinth, but the serenity stayed with him. He changed his tunic, musing about his renewed hope, before going to find some breakfast. His mother had loved him. Somehow that made all the difference.

But then he stepped inside the dining hall.

Yakob and his friends had gathered around one large table, laughing and joking while they ate their breakfast. The apprentices nudged one another and smirked when they saw him. "Sleep well?" Yakob called out.

Haefen nodded, his stomach in a knot. He surveyed the dining hall, then turned on his heel and left. He wasn't hungry any more. If he were blessed, the apprentices would think he'd already eaten and had come by searching for someone. Laurelin, perhaps.

His finger throbbed. It was still twice its normal size, and now it was black and blue besides. He'd stop by the house of healing. That might give him time to regain his calm.

The meeting with Brother Efrat started out well, at least. He beamed at Haefen, praising him for Brother Biorn's glowing report on his progress. Haefen perched on his chair and forced himself to smile. Soon Brother Efrat would get to the part where he said none of that mattered, since Haefen still didn't know his father's name.

Brother Efrat frowned. "Is something wrong, Haefen? You've lost your sense of peace."

Haefen shrugged. "I'm glad I did well in my apprenticeship, thanks to Brother Biorn's guidance, but I know that isn't enough."

"Your father's name. I was getting to that." Brother Efrat leaned back in his chair. "I located the description of a ring in the histories. A unique ring, the craftsmanship impossible to duplicate because of its legendary origin. Its description matches the ring on your finger. May I see it again?"

Haefen hesitated. The swelling had gone down after his visit to the house of healing, but his finger was still bruised. He didn't want Brother Efrat to see it and ask questions.

Then he remembered what Brother Biorn had taught him. Haefen stroked the ring, commanding it in a breath, and slid it off his finger. He set it on the desk.

Brother Efrat turned the ring in his hand, tracing the golden spiral. "Yes, this matches the description of the ring King Beraqel was wont to wear. I searched all week, but the histories don't mention the ring after Queen Elin fled for her life with an enclave of Puerán. Historians had always supposed the ring went with the king to his grave, or that the Sons of Darkness confiscated it when they executed him. Obviously we've been mistaken. I asked Brother Fredrik if he knew of a family tradition that accounted for the ring's disappearance, but he knew no more than I did.

"The Domarring wasn't built until King Beraqel had long been dead and dust, and we can't know how long the ring lay under the altar in the stone circle. But I'm certain you were directed to find the ring. It chooses to fit your finger, just as it chose to fit the king's finger. It recognized you, Haefen. So, even though you don't know your father's name, I'd advise you to use the king's name when you face the wall of the Qodesh."

Haefen gaped at Brother Efrat.

"Beraqel must be a distant relation of yours, Haefen. Perhaps you're descended from a cousin, or some such thing. The connection is close enough that the ring recognized you, so the Qodesh may as well. Your lineage is a worthy one, whoever your father and mother may have been."

Haefen floated out of Brother Efrat's office, bursting with a joy that pushed aside his fears. He grinned and twisted the ring. The circle in a circle. If only he could thank the traveler who'd given his foster father that note.

Haefen would ascend the spiraling path and step through the wall of the Qodesh, just as he'd always dreamed he would. He would receive the power that awaited him there. And then he would dedicate his life to Abba El. Somehow. How else could he give thanks for such a surfeit of joy?

Haefen had planned to fast after breakfast, to strengthen his spirit before facing the Qodesh. So it'd be foolish to eat now, as late as it was. He'd rather practice his skills.

He stopped by the cottage where he'd met with Brother Biorn, to fetch the candle and the stone. Any stone would have worked, but after staring at it for so many hours, Haefen had grown fond of this one. On impulse he picked up The Book of the Faithful lying beside the rug.

He turned to a passage he'd read many times back home in Phonteh. "Hanoch spake in the name of Ben El, and the mountains moved; rivers of water turned out of their course to defend his people."

Peace washed over him. The power to move mountains. Haefen had a taste of that power, but he'd have so much more once he entered the Qodesh. His capacity to serve Abba El had already been enlarged, but tomorrow it might expand beyond anything he could imagine. If the king's name were enough.

Where to go? Haefen wanted to practice somewhere secluded, but outside. He rejected the clearing where Brother Biorn had taken him. Anyone might wander out of the dining hall.

The sheep pen. There'd been a grove of trees beyond it, and not much else.

Haefen followed the path northward. The workshops were deserted and silent, the fields empty. Everyone else was spending the day with their families. Though Laurelin didn't have a family. His footsteps slowed.

He needed to practice, whatever else happened today. He wanted to add confidence to his hope. But after his practice, he'd go and find Laurelin. He smiled. He'd invite Laurelin to his sacrifice tomorrow, and apologize for abandoning her at the dance.

Haefen hopped over the fence and greeted the sheep the way Brother Biorn had taught him. It would be harder to communicate with animals away from the Shechinah. But these sheep crowded around, baaing and butting their heads into Haefen's legs, begging to have their ears scratched. Haefen laughed. They were as friendly as dogs.

But the grove beckoned. Haefen clambered over the fence at the far side of the sheep pen, and strode under the beech trees, searching for a good spot. He found a small clearing near the center of the grove that was perfect.

He knelt on the leaves under the light of the Shechinah, and dedicated his heart to Abba El. "Please find me worthy. Please help me prepare to enter the Qodesh. And please let the king's name suffice in place of my father's. I want to serve thee, to be a powerful tool in thine hands."

Haefen cleared away the leaf litter and placed the candle and the stone on the bare dirt. He sat cross-legged and focused his mind and his heart. It only took a moment after his week of practice.

The candle filled his gaze. He'd lit it so many times already, but never outside. Haefen leaned toward it and blew, giving it the breath of life. And the wick flared. A breeze blew through the clearing, but the candle burned on.

The stone was another matter. All week it'd been more difficult to move the stone than to light the candle. He studied it, letting the stone fill his mind. It should be simple. It was simple. With a flick of his hand, he sent the stone over the burning candle to settle in the dirt on the other side. He grinned.

Then he refocused, aligning his heart and mind with Abba El. Haefen held out his hand, palm up. He wasn't sure how this would work in the open air, but he tilted back his head and gazed into the Shechinah, asking it to fill the clearing with the light of Ben El.

The air brightened around him, white and glorious, like white fire. It took Haefen's breath away, filling his heart with light, blazing through his mind. The light fed his soul.

Haefen blew out the candle and lay full length in the clearing, surrounded by the glorious, white light. He'd felt connected to Piqqeah in the labyrinth, watching her spiral through the universe with the other planets.

It was either impossible, or it was simple.

The leaves above him trembled in the breeze. Haefen closed his eyes and dug his fingers into the dirt. He spiraled deeper within himself until he found his center. His inner stillness.

Lighting the candle was simple. Moving the stone was simple. Even talking to sheep was simple. Folding the dirt was simple too.

Haefen sent his heart searching for Piqqeah's soul.

He pictured the rug in the empty cottage. He'd spent many hours there this week, sitting across from Brother Biorn. It was a familiar spot. A welcoming spot. Haefen's heart touched another's. He breathed in the light of Ben El. Exhaled. And sat up on the rug.

Haefen didn't know he could feel this happy. His eyes welled up with tears. Dropping to his knees, he poured out his thanks to Abba El.

39

Aron eased the front door shut and hurried back down the path toward the center of the community. Part of the morning had gone well, at least. His mother had been delighted when he told her he'd danced with Olivia.

Qanaah would be sad when she realized he'd left so soon after the midday meal, but Aron couldn't bear to be around his father any longer. Fredrik was still grumbling that Aron refused to face the Qodesh on the morrow. He probably wouldn't stop until Haefen returned to his village.

Aron heard the other apprentices before he saw them. He came around the House of Light and found them in the field on the far side, rolling around in the grass. They had wrestling competitions every Saturday, though Aron usually gave them a miss. He had enough of the others' fawning during the week. But maybe wrestling would take the edge off his frustration.

Most of the apprentices knelt in the grass, cheering on the two who rolled around in the center of the group. They shouted advice, and argued about who would win, too caught up in the fight to notice Aron's approach.

Yakob and Jarom were deep in conversation. "Another minute and I would have had the ring off his finger. Too bad those brothers came along right then."

"At least we put Haefen in his place," Jarom said.

Yakob chuckled. "Face first in the dirt." He choked off when he noticed Aron behind them.

Aron kept his voice even, though it was a struggle.

"What's this about Haefen's ring?"

Yakob swallowed. "Brother Fredrik, your father, explained how Haefen desecrated an altar and stole your ring."

"My ring?"

Yakob's face reddened. "Brother Fredrik said he'd let you wear the ring, Aron. If we got it back."

Aron snorted. "So you assaulted an apprentice in training, a guest in our community, in my name."

He turned on his heel and strode back to the path, clenching and unclenching his fists. He'd go to the combat school and try out the heavier practice sword Master Long had found for him. And then Aron would find Haefen and apologize. He could explain that he'd had nothing to do with the boys' abuse.

In truth, Aron shouldn't be angry at the other apprentices. His father had put them up to it. Fredrik was the one who'd brought shame on their family name.

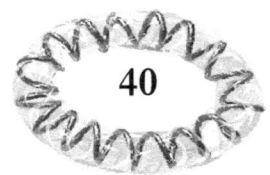

40

Laurelin's eyes lit up when Haefen found her outside the dining hall. He caught his breath. She was so beautiful when she smiled like that. And the dance didn't matter. Her eyes hadn't shone while she danced with Aron.

"Hi, Laurelin."

"Hey. I thought you'd be studying all day today."

He shrugged. "I'm as ready as I'm going to be."

"That's great. I know how worried you were."

"Would you like to attend my sacrifice in the morning, Laurelin? And walk beside me to the wall of the Qodesh? I don't have any family here, so I hoped you might stand in their place."

"Of course I would. I'd love to."

Haefen smiled. "Brother Efrat will send someone to wake you. We need to be standing in front of the Qodesh at dawn."

"I'll be ready."

"Do you have time for a walk right now?"

"Sure. It's been a whole week since we went on our last little jaunt." She wiggled her feet in the shoes he'd made her. "Where do you want to go?"

"I'd like to follow the stream that flows through the center of the community. Viktor said there's a waterfall at the southern end, spilling off the edge of the plateau."

They started at the water clock and followed the center path southward. The stream chattered in its stone-lined bed, coursing along the middle of the cobblestone path. Haefen itched to take Laurelin's hand, but he didn't have the courage.

Another path intersected theirs. Aron strode along it, deep in thought. And wearing his blue-sleeved tunic, of course. Haefen bit his lip.

Aron saw them and stopped short, his face flushed. "I just heard what happened last night, Haefen. I want you to know I didn't initiate it, and I'm sorry. My father...." Aron trailed off and shook his head. "My father wants to be the king's heir in truth. He thinks it's time to retake Betavar, before Mahan can finish consolidating his position. He thinks I'll be leading an army to victory over the Sons of Darkness. That all I need to succeed is to do everything King Beraqel did. Wear his ring, recover his armor." Aron sighed. "Anyway, I'm sorry."

Laurelin glanced from Haefen to Aron, and back. "What happened last night?"

Haefen twisted the ring and smiled. "It doesn't matter. Aron had nothing to do with it."

"Thank you, Haefen, for your forgiveness." Aron hesitated. "Could I ask you a favor?"

Haefen shrugged. "If you'd like."

"I thought you might know how to fight with a staff, since you come from a farming village. Master Long has sparred with me, staff against sword, but I'd like to try my sword against someone besides a combat master. Just a friendly match."

Haefen pictured Aron's whirling sword from Monday night. He'd never fought anyone who had that much skill.

Laurelin grinned. "I'd love to see you guys duel it out. I missed the combat demonstration, you know."

What could Haefen say to that? "I'd like to see how a staff fares against a sword, but I'll be leaving for home on the morning after the Sabbath. We'd have to fight now, if that's all right."

Aron grinned. "That's perfect. I was just on my way to the combat school."

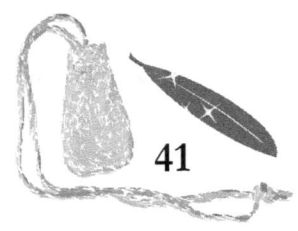

41

Laurelin was sandwiched between Haefen and Aron as they strode toward the combat school. She couldn't wipe the grin from her face. She'd seen movie fights, of course. And rigged gladiator fights on television. But she'd never seen people really dueling with weapons.

Aron was taller than Haefen, so he'd have a longer reach. But a staff was longer than a sword, wasn't it? She pictured Haefen fighting off a sword with a broom handle, and having it chopped into bits. She chuckled. That would only happen in a movie.

They arrived at the combat school. Aron swung open the gate and ushered them into a courtyard, then led them to a door on the far side. A man put down the wooden sword he'd been oiling when they entered. Laurelin hadn't known that some of the Puerán looked Asian. How did Chinese people get to Piqqeah?

Aron bowed to the man. "Master Long, Haefen has agreed to spar with me, staff against sword. Would you be willing to mediate?"

Master Long returned the bow. "Gladly. It will be good practice for you both."

He found a staff for Haefen in the back of a cupboard, a thick piece of bamboo as long as Haefen was tall. "This is a practice staff, Haefen. A battle staff would be made from the heart of an oak tree, and fire hardened. It could crush Aron's skull like an egg."

Haefen bowed and took the staff. "Thank you, Master Long."

Aron grabbed a wooden sword out of a bin, and he and Haefen stepped onto the practice floor and faced one another. They bowed, their eyes never leaving the other's face, and raised their weapons.

Laurelin picked a spot along the wall, halfway between them, and leaned back to enjoy the show.

Aron swung his sword. Haefen pivoted, and the end of his staff smacked into Aron's ribs so that he grunted, caught off balance.

Aron faced him again, but Haefen's staff darted past Aron's sword and swept his ankle out from under him. Aron rolled and came up with his sword at the ready.

The staff was a more effective weapon than Laurelin had expected. She smiled. Haefen was holding his own.

Haefen attacked and Aron struggled to block the blows. The longer staff gave Haefen greater reach and versatility. He could bind up Aron's sword with one end, then press the attack with the other before Aron had time to respond.

But Aron got in his strikes, as well. When Haefen hesitated once, Aron smacked his wrists. Another time, Aron grabbed the staff before Haefen could raise it to block, and stabbed Haefen's abdomen several times in a row.

Haefen's staff wasn't fast enough to counter Aron's sword all the time. Some of the attacks landed on Haefen's ribs with a loud thwack. He'd have some bruises.

Minutes went by. Aron slowed. Blocking the blows from the heavier staff must have been tiring.

Finally, Haefen deflected Aron's blade with a twist of his staff and smacked Aron's wrist hard enough to bruise. His practice sword went flying.

Haefen grounded the butt of his staff against the practice floor and bowed to Aron. "That was a good match," he said.

Aron laughed and returned the bow. "That was amazing. I learned even more than I expected." He turned to Master Long. "Master, can you teach me how to wield a staff that well? Think how formidable I'd be knowing both sword and staff."

Master Long nodded. "An excellent idea."

"We'll leave you to practice," Haefen said. He and Laurelin took their leave and strolled back toward the stream in the center of the community.

Laurelin gave Haefen a sidelong glance as they walked. He was good at everything he set his hand to. Trapping animals and skinning them, sewing her moccasins. Even smacking someone around with a pole. And he still had that adorably crooked smile. "That was a great fight, Haefen," she said.

He shrugged. "I was glad to hold my own. Aron is adept with a sword."

"It was just a piece of wood."

"Better than being sliced into ribbons," he said, rubbing his ribs. "Do we still have time to find the waterfall? Or do you need to be somewhere?"

Laurelin smiled. "I don't need to be anywhere until morning."

42

Haefen lay in bed with his hands behind his head, smiling at the ceiling. Disarming Aron had been incredibly satisfying, even though he hadn't been responsible for what the other apprentices had done.

But the waterfall had been better, and as spectacular as Viktor had said. Haefen and Laurelin had followed the chattering stream in its stone-lined channel until it cut through a cleft in the hills and vanished into a mist.

The path continued down a series of steps the Puerán had cut into the edge of the plateau, though the brothers hadn't bothered to add a railing. Haefen had climbed down, hugging the rock wall, with Laurelin close behind. The steps led them behind the waterfall to a damp ledge with a bench carved out of the rock. They'd sat there for the longest time, mesmerized by the falling water, until their hair clung to their heads in damp tendrils, and their clothes were soaked.

The thundering waterfall had been too loud for them to hear each other speak. But Haefen had felt closer to Laurelin on that stone bench than all during their trek to Mount Nevo. They'd grinned at one another and shook their heads, awestruck by the magnificence of Abba El's creation.

But tomorrow he'd face the Qodesh, and then it would be time to go home. Laurelin had said she'd journey with him, but that wouldn't help her return to her own home. She'd be better off staying with the Puerán on Mount Nevo.

Though Haefen would miss her when he left.

But first he'd walk through the wall of the Qodesh and receive the power that awaited him there. The glorious power of Abba El. Mighty enough to move mountains and turn rivers out of their course, and compassionate enough to let him see a vision of his mother cradling him in love.

Haefen rolled onto his side and pictured his mother as he'd seen her in the labyrinth. She'd held him. She'd loved him. He smiled and snuggled his head into the pillow. His name was Haefen, and tomorrow he would invoke the king's name and walk through the wall of the Qodesh.

The next moment, he was asleep.

He awoke in darkness, the light of the Shechinah gone, and an acrid odor in the air. He sniffed. It stunk like burning hair.

Haefen sat up, his heart racing, as chanting voices surrounded him on every side. He couldn't understand the words, but the sound of them throbbed in his head like a heartbeat. Insistent, unceasing.

Then one voice called out in clear, ringing tones, "Prince of Darkness, hear us now! Uncover the hidden treasure. Let us find what we seek."

The Sons of Darkness?

Haefen's finger burned. The ring glowed red in the darkness, the golden spiral shining like sunlight on his bruised finger. The voices grew louder, clearer, and the ring burned hotter, like the heat of a forge.

A face appeared in the darkness. A man stood at the end of Haefen's bed, swathed in a dark robe. He was bald, except for a gold-laced braid running back from his forehead and over the top of his head. A necklace of finger bones embellished the front of his robe, strung on a gold chain with a twig wedged in the center. The braid, the finger bones, the twig. This was the High Priest of the Sons of the Prince. Mahan was his name.

He grinned at Haefen with teeth stained red. "You have

something that belongs to us, young one." Mahan stretched out his hand. "Give me the ring."

Haefen sat up straighter. "Why should I? You have no power over me. Your glory is darkness, and I worship the light."

Haefen raised his right hand, the ring blazing above him like a shooting star. With the tip of his forefinger, he inscribed a flaming spiral in the air. He called out in a loud voice, "Servants of the dark Prince, I rebuke you in the name of Ben El!"

The sound of his voice rang through the darkness, shattering it. Light, the blessed light of the Shechinah, surrounded him. Enfolded him. Haefen sat on his bed and waited for his breathing to slow and his limbs to stop their trembling.

The other boys slept on, oblivious.

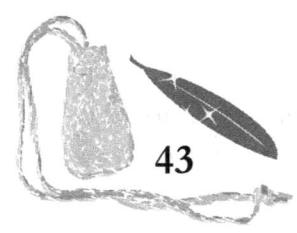

43

Sister Nora awakened Laurelin hours before dawn, and led her to where the brothers waited outside Haefen's dormitory. Eleven men stood there, clumped together on the path. One had a blue-sleeved tunic just like Aron's. That must be Aron's dad.

Brother Efrat led a rumpled Haefen out of the dormitory, and they all traipsed after them to where the House of Washing stood nestled amongst the trees.

It was a small square building, surrounded by a small square moat. The brothers and Haefen crossed a narrow bridge and entered, shutting the door behind them. Laurelin and Sister Nora were left to wait outside.

Laurelin yawned and leaned against the end of the bridge railing. "Why is there water around the building?"

Sister Nora rubbed her bare arms against the chilly air. "When we cross the bridge, we recommit ourselves to the promises we made to Abba El in the Qodesh, as if the water cleanses our spirits. Inside the House of Washing, the brothers will purify Haefen for when he makes his own promises today."

"So girls do this, too? I mean, like Olivia?"

"Yes. When Olivia is ready to be an Iysha, the sisters will lead her here and cleanse her in the same way. She'll be anointed with miriel, as will Haefen, and then perform the sacrifice."

"What's miriel?"

Sister Nora's eyebrows rose. "You don't have the flower

of Abba El in your land?"

"No." Laurelin's hand strayed to the pouch around her neck. "I guess not."

"We gather miriel flowers on the mountaintops, and grind them into powder for our worship of Abba El. The brothers will anoint Haefen with miriel powder as they would a sacrifice, because Haefen is offering his life in service to Abba El."

That was the second time Sister Nora had mentioned a sacrifice. Laurelin shuddered. She hoped Haefen wasn't going to slaughter an animal or something. His snares had been bad enough.

Her mind drifted to the day before. The waterfall had been stunning. Watching it cascade past the hollow where she and Haefen sat had been like something out of a movie. And kind of like a date. She smiled just thinking about it.

It was peaceful outside the House of Washing. The Shechinah shone brighter here than elsewhere in the community, except for maybe inside the House of Light.

The door opened and Brother Efrat stepped out, followed by Haefen and the others. Laurelin stepped away from the bridge to let them pass.

Sister Nora smiled. "I'll leave you now Laurelin, but I'll see you at Sabbath service. You too, Haefen. May your new life be filled with joy."

She turned and left, and Haefen stepped over beside Laurelin. His head was shaved bare, and his tunic was pure white instead of the usual cream color. His forehead was smeared with a bright yellow streak, just like when she'd first met him at the stone circle.

Haefen looked different without his hair. Older or something.

"So what's this about a sacrifice?" Laurelin asked.

Haefen smiled. "We go there now."

They followed the brothers through the trees to a small,

square clearing north of the House of Washing. Stones had been piled in the center with a flat stone set on top, just like the stone table in the House of Light. One of the brothers handed Haefen a tray, then went to stand along the edge of the clearing with the others, three on a side.

"Laurelin," Brother Efrat said, motioning her over. "Stand by me while Haefen places his offering on the altar."

So that was an altar. But Laurelin didn't see an animal anywhere. She crossed her fingers.

Haefen set the tray on the altar stone, then knelt and bowed his head. The brothers bowed their heads, too, so Laurelin did the same.

"Abba El," Haefen said, "I kneel before thee and acknowledge my debt for breath and strength. I'm grateful for my life and my many blessings, especially that I may approach thy most holy place. In the name of Ben El, amen."

Laurelin raised her head when Brother Efrat did. Haefen rose to his feet, then took a knife from the tray and slit the tip of his left thumb. Laurelin winced.

Haefen's voice rang through the clearing. "In the name of Ben El, I offer my life in thy service." He smeared his bleeding thumb on the corners of the altar stone, then picked up a cup. Dipping the tip of his right forefinger into the cup, he drew a yellow spiral on top of the altar. "Please sanctify me to thy service, and grant me fellowship with thee." He bent and touched his forehead to the spiral.

Brother Efrat stepped forward and faced Haefen across the altar. He placed his right palm on the center of the spiral and said, "I accept your offering in the name of Ben El." Then he poured a few drops of oil on Haefen's spiral.

Haefen leaned closer and blew on the liquid. It burst into flame, flaring brightly before burning out.

Brother Efrat smiled. "Well done, Haefen."

"Thank you." He grinned.

Brother Efrat turned and strode out of the clearing

along a path leading further north. The other brothers followed, all in a line, with Haefen and Laurelin hurrying behind.

No one spoke.

The path turned west, then entered a tunnel at the base of Mount Nevo's tallest peak. It looked just like the tunnel leading to the Miphtan, but narrower so that they had to walk single file. Small embrasures had been set into the outer wall every few feet, so that the tunnel was flooded with the light of the Shechinah.

The tunnel wound its way around and around the narrow peak, climbing ever higher in a spiraling path. Half an hour passed and Laurelin's calves ached, but the view was amazing. The Puerán community lay far below them, like a toy village.

But she couldn't stand the silence any longer. She caught up to Haefen and whispered, "I didn't know they'd shave your head. Do they shave girls when they get washed?"

Haefen glanced back, smiling his crooked smile. "No."

"Are you nervous?"

"I'm hopeful," he whispered. "Whatever happens will be as Abba El wishes. Thank you for sharing this day with me, Laurelin."

"I wouldn't have missed it."

The tunnel's spiral tightened, and Laurelin's breath grew labored. She stared at her feet, plodding upward one weary step after another. They had to be nearing the summit soon.

The tunnel opened out onto a small plateau, but they hadn't reached the summit. The peak soared above them still, to the west, barren of trees and covered in snow. Laurelin shivered.

An arched stone bridge crossed the chasm between their plateau and a square cave, cut into the side of the peak. The cave glowed brighter than the sky outside it, as if the Shechinah began inside the cave. The Qodesh portico.

The brothers marched across the bridge, into the

portico, and into the square wall on the far side, all without pausing. They vanished one by one into the rock.

"They'll wait for me inside," Haefen said.

Laurelin followed him across the narrow bridge. She glanced down once, and regretted it. The chasm was at least five hundred feet deep. And the portico had no railing. Laurelin sat near the back wall, as far from the edge as she could. But the edge was still only four feet away. Too bad she couldn't walk through the wall and wait inside with the brothers.

Had Brother Efrat told the other brothers Haefen didn't know his father's name? Aron's dad had frowned at Haefen the whole time in the clearing with the altar. And before stepping through the wall of the Qodesh, he'd glanced over his shoulder and frowned again.

Laurelin shivered and blew on her hands. It didn't get dark here, but the sun still hadn't risen and the air was cool this high up. Her stomach felt like one big knot. This was it. She was nervous for Haefen, but excitement bubbled through her as well.

The square portico opening framed a view of the distant horizon. The Shechinah filled the top third, but below the glowing cloud was a dark, predawn sky.

The sky lightened while Laurelin watched, pink light spreading through the darkness as the morning sun neared the edge of the horizon.

Haefen stood beside her with his back to the Qodesh wall, waiting for sunrise.

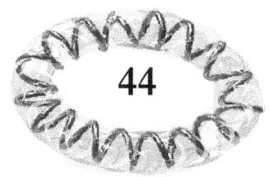

44

Haefen tensed when he saw the brothers walk through the wall of the Qodesh. They made it look so easy, as if it weren't even there. And soon it would be his turn.

The air was chilly on his newly shaved head, even in the Qodesh portico where they were protected from the breeze. Laurelin sat near the wall, rubbing her arms for warmth. He should have brought his blanket for her to wrap herself in while she waited. "I'm not sure how long I'll be inside," he said.

"I don't mind. I'm just glad we're here."

Haefen's stomach rumbled.

Laurelin chuckled. "Time for breakfast?"

"Almost." It had been a day and a half since his last meal, but he was too anxious to feel hungry.

Haefen stared eastward, waiting. The sun was close to rising. The horizon was pink now.

Somewhere in that direction lay Asseldam, and Mahan, High Priest of the Sons of Darkness. Why had they wanted the king's ring? And would they try for it again? Haefen had vanquished the Sons once, and he would be even stronger after he was armed with the power of the Qodesh. He spun the ring around his finger, the golden spiral twirling in a never-ending helix.

He'd almost told Brother Efrat about the Sons' attack when he came to wake him. But then Brother Efrat might have wanted to take the ring, and Haefen needed it to enter the Qodesh. Even if all it did was remind him of his heritage. He was related to King Beraqel, Betavar's last king. A distant cousin or something, but still.

Rohbert and Rute would be astonished when Haefen told them. He'd be glad to return home. Though, he'd probably never see Laurelin again. That would be the cup of sadness that seasoned his joy.

The sun edged above the horizon, and a ray of light shone on Haefen's face. He pulled off his shoes and turned to face the Qodesh. The ring clicked against the rock when he placed his hands on the wall. He heard a voice in his mind, a gentle voice that pierced his soul.

"Who approaches my sanctuary?"

The wall warmed beneath his cold hands. Haefen swallowed. "Haefen Ben Beraqel." His heart thudded in his chest. He'd felt peaceful until this moment, but what if the king's name weren't enough?

Had he failed? His years of preparation, his long journey, his exhausting week. Were they all in vain without his father's name? Tears shone in his eyes. He would take his baby blanket to every village and ask if anyone recognized it. Someone must remember his mother and her child. He would search as long as it took. He would find his father's name and return.

Haefen sucked in his breath when the wall dissolved beneath his fingers.

The voice whispered, "Come."

Haefen had thought that entering the Qodesh would feel like passing through the wall of the Miphtan. Instead he felt a tugging on his heart, as if a string had been looped around it.

He stepped forward, floating into a vast, dark space. A pinprick of white light glowed in the darkness beyond. The light grew as he moved toward it, following the tug on his heart like a kite on a string. Forward. Onward.

The light grew until it swallowed the darkness, encompassing him with its radiance. Haefen stood in an immense hall, more magnificent than any building he'd ever seen. The ceiling soared high above him. White light filled the hall, bright after the darkness. His eyes watered and Haefen blinked away the tears. Joy filled him like the light filled the hall, permeating every particle of his soul.

The brothers waited, standing in an arc. Some of them had been surprised to see him. Not Brother Efrat, but some of the others. They must've heard that Haefen didn't know his father's name.

Brother Efrat stood in the center of the arc. He took a step back and to the side, gesturing for Haefen to step through the line of brothers and kneel at the altar behind them.

The ceremony that followed was so intense and uplifting that Haefen's joy overflowed. The light tasted sweet, and his spirit burned within him.

Brother Efrat helped Haefen up and handed him a tiny auger hanging from a chain. "Always remember whose hand is on the auger, Haefen. The spiral turns according to his design." He slipped the chain over Haefen's head and tucked the auger down the front of his white tunic. Pressing his hand over the hidden auger, Brother Efrat looked into Haefen's eyes. "Be a voice for the truth, and a lens for his light."

Then Brother Efrat wrapped his arms around Haefen, and hugged him like a father. "Congratulations."

Haefen felt so buoyant. He was surprised he wasn't floating through the hall. Maybe he'd been fasting too long.

The Puerán had furnished the rest of the enormous hall with magnificent paintings, sculptures, and luxurious furnishings. Brother Efrat showed him all the treasures. Some of the things had been rescued from Betavar, and others had been created in the hundreds of years since. They'd all been made with the finest craftsmanship. The Qodesh was a house worthy of Abba El.

A crystal chest rested on the stone floor in the corner farthest from the altar. Brother Efrat gazed at it for a moment in silence. "This chest holds King Beraqel's breastplate, Haefen. Queen Elin sealed it in the chest with her own hands. It's sat here ever since, waiting for when the king's heir is prepared to recover the kingdom.

"The histories say that Elin's son Reuel expected the chest to open when he grew to manhood and entered the Qodesh, but it didn't. Nor did it open for Reuel's son, or his grandson, and so on down the centuries."

The breastplate had white, overlapping scales. It fascinated Haefen. It was so different from any other armor he'd seen. "So some day the Puerán will overthrow the Sons of Darkness and reclaim Betavar?" Maybe Aron would end up with a kingdom after all.

Haefen crouched down to get a closer look at the breastplate through the front of the crystal chest.

The crystal shattered in a line across the front, and the chest opened, the lid rising of its own accord.

Haefen cringed. Shards of glass littered the floor. He'd broken the chest, the Puerán's greatest treasure. He turned to Brother Efrat, but Brother Efrat ignored him, staring open mouthed into the chest.

Someone behind them gasped, then Brother Fredrik surged forward, pushing Haefen out of the way. He rubbed his hands together, then reached into the chest.

Haefen saw Brother Fredrik's hand through the crystal, reaching for the breastplate. But his hand passed through it. Brother Fredrik fell on his knees in front of the chest and felt all along the bottom, and even the sides. Nothing. His efforts became frantic.

Brother Efrat put his arm around Brother Fredrik's shoulders. "I'm sorry, my friend, but it's not meant to be. Step back for a moment."

"Do you think it's meant for Aron, then?" A glint of

hope brightened Brother Fredrik's gaze.

"We can't know until Aron prepares himself to enter the Qodesh."

The other Puerán had gathered from around the hall. They surrounded the chest, marveling at the breastplate, crowding Haefen out of the way.

He stood behind them, listening to excited whispers about what the open chest might mean.

"Come here, Haefen," Brother Efrat said, making a path for him through the midst of the brothers.

Haefen hesitated, but stepped forward. "Whatever I did, I'm sorry. I didn't mean to."

Brother Efrat chuckled. "I'm sure you didn't. Pick up the breastplate, Haefen."

"What?" Brother Fredrik shouted.

Brother Efrat held up a hand. "Remember where we are."

"But, you can't mean that you think...." Brother Fredrik spluttered. "The king's ring was ridiculous enough. This is blasphemy."

Brother Efrat raised an eyebrow, but didn't reply. "Haefen, pick up the breastplate," he repeated.

But Haefen was unnerved by Brother Fredrik's wild eyes, and he didn't want to upset him further.

Brother Efrat put a hand on Haefen's shoulder. "You must try."

So Haefen reached into the chest with his trembling right hand, the ring glinting in the white light. He jerked back when he felt the smooth, hard texture of the breastplate under his fingers.

"Pick it up, Haefen," Brother Efrat said.

Haefen bit his lip, but reached in with both hands and lifted the breastplate out of the chest. The brothers backed away, exclaiming in surprise.

The breastplate weighed so little, but it was solid in

Haefen's hands. The white light of the Qodesh sent rainbows flickering across the facets of two clear stones, set into the scales at chest level. Haefen gaped. The breastplate shone with a glory from beyond his world.

The crystal chest had obscured the breastplate's splendor for generations. The brothers were wide-eyed, and as entranced as Haefen.

Except for Brother Fredrik. He shook with shock and anger. His teeth were clenched in his red face, and he glared at Haefen with murder in his eyes.

Haefen whirled and put the breastplate back inside the chest. He pressed the lid shut and stepped back, his heart thudding.

Brother Fredrik shoved him out of the way. He struggled to open the chest, but it had sealed itself shut. Even the crystal shards had vanished from the floor. He muttered and half cried in frustration, rubbing his hands along the front and sides of the chest.

"Come away from the chest," Brother Efrat said. "It is time we left the sanctuary."

Brother Fredrik opened his mouth to speak, but Brother Efrat hushed him. The other Puerán murmured, eyeing Haefen with bewildered faces.

Brother Efrat strode off, leading them all back through the wall of the Qodesh.

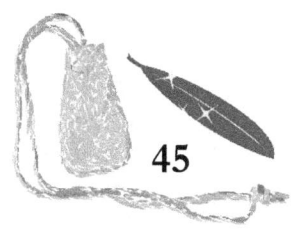

45

Laurelin couldn't stop smiling after Haefen stepped into the rock. He'd done it. Walked through the wall of the Qodesh with his yellow forehead and his bald head. She couldn't imagine how happy he must feel.

But it was still cold in the Qodesh portico. And after a few minutes, she started to feel left out.

Laurelin scooted into the back corner and leaned against the warm Qodesh wall. The sunlight felt glorious on her face. She'd gotten used to the Shechinah, but she'd missed the sun. She closed her eyes and soaked it in.

The light shone red through her closed eyelids. It reminded her of all the lazy days she'd spent at the beach with her friends. Friends in California she'd probably never see again.

Two weeks ago that thought would have made her angry, and she would have raged at her dad for dragging her to Missouri. But now? She shrugged. All her anger had dissipated somewhere on Piqqeah.

Laurelin still didn't have any friends in Missouri, but she could make some. Once she got back. She was bound to meet people when school started, and until then she had the church group. Not that she planned to spend time with geeky Gregory from next door. But some of the other people in the group might be interesting. There might be someone like Olivia, or even Aron.

Laurelin dozed off, huddled against the warm rock.

"This is an outrage!" a man shouted.

Laurelin blinked and rubbed her eyes. Haefen and the brothers had emerged from the Qodesh wall.

Aron's dad stood in front of Brother Efrat, waving his arms in his blue-sleeved tunic. "You must do something, Brother Efrat!"

Brother Efrat rested his hands on the man's shoulders. "Calm yourself, Brother Fredrik."

"Calm myself?" Brother Fredrik's face grew even redder.

Laurelin shrank back into her corner.

Brother Efrat glanced toward the smooth rock wall of the Qodesh. "We'll discuss this after we return to the community, Brother Fredrik." He stepped onto the bridge, crossing back toward the plateau and the tunnel opening beyond it.

The other brothers followed, with Brother Fredrik last of all. He glared at Haefen before he left the portico, then kicked Haefen's shoes into the chasm far below.

Laurelin gaped.

When the brothers had all disappeared into the tunnel, Haefen folded his legs and sat beside her. "Caught you sleeping on the job." His words were light, but his voice sounded strained.

"What happened?"

"I'm not sure. I was so happy, and now...." Haefen shook his head.

"Tell me about it from the beginning. I mean, at least the stuff you're allowed to talk about."

Haefen stared at his knees. "We had a ceremony at the altar, and then Brother Efrat showed me around the hall. The Qodesh is immense, Laurelin, and so beautiful. And the light. The light inside the Qodesh is a piece of heaven."

Haefen's face glowed, and Laurelin felt left out again. She'd never see what Haefen had seen, feel what he'd felt.

"There's a crystal chest at the back of the hall. King

Beraqel's breastplate is sealed inside, waiting for the king's heir to claim it and fight to retake Betavar from the Sons of Darkness."

Haefen swallowed. "But Laurelin, the crystal chest opened when I stood in front of it. Brother Fredrik tried to take the breastplate out of the chest, but he couldn't touch it. So Brother Efrat told me to pick it up. And I did." Haefen's voice trailed off. "I don't know what to think."

No wonder Brother Fredrik had been so mad. Laurelin's stomach rumbled. She stood and reached for Haefen's hand. "Let's go eat breakfast. Maybe all this will make more sense after you've eaten."

Haefen let her pull him up. "I am a bit lightheaded."

Laurelin crossed the bridge first. She glanced over the railing, but Haefen's shoes had been swallowed by the chasm. He took the lead when they entered the tunnel, Haefen in his bare feet and Laurelin in her moccasins.

46

Aron hid in the trees near the Qodesh tunnel entrance, too curious to wait until Sabbath service to find out how Haefen had done. Aron could have been with Haefen, stood beside him. They could have walked through the wall of the Qodesh together.

But Aron didn't regret his decision. He would enter the Qodesh when the time felt right, and this wasn't it.

The tunnel gaped invitingly. Aron had crept up the spiraling path more than once when he was younger, dared by the other boys. But he'd never made it as far as the plateau. Long before that, his footsteps would slow, and his thundering heart would send him pelting back down the path. Abba El had no need of locked doors.

He heard voices echoing through the tunnel windows. Haefen had finished, then. About time. Although the voices were loud for the Sabbath.

Aron ducked behind a tree so only his eyes showed through a screen of leaves.

Brother Efrat emerged from the tunnel in a rush. He probably had a meeting before Sabbath service. He stopped short, however, when he drew even with Aron's hiding place.

Aron held his breath.

Brother Efrat didn't scan the trees, didn't even turn his head. "Aron," he said, "I need you to do me a service."

Giving service was better than being chastised. Aron pushed through the trees and onto the path. "How can I serve you, Brother Efrat?"

A knot of men burst from the tunnel before Brother

Efrat could speak, Aron's father among them. Aron's heart sank. The brothers' faces were grim, and Haefen was nowhere to be seen. Had he failed?

"You!" his father yelled, stomping up to Aron. "This is your fault. If you'd been there, none of this would have happened. And look at you." He tugged on Aron's cream-colored sleeve. "You're a disgrace to your family. No wonder you've been passed over."

"Brother Fredrik!" Brother Efrat's eyes flashed. "This is not the time or the place." He turned to Aron. "That service I spoke of. I need you to retrieve Haefen and Laurelin's belongings and bring them to Brother Sigurd's clearing. Quickly, now."

"Of course." Aron spun around and ran toward the dormitories. Anything to get away from his father when he was angry.

Aron grabbed Haefen's pack from his dormitory and ran to Laurelin's. Olivia answered the door when he knocked. She hurried and gathered Laurelin's belongings, and handed him the bag. But Aron couldn't tell her why Brother Efrat needed them.

Something had happened at the Qodesh. That much was obvious. And because of it, Brother Sigurd would lead Haefen down the stone hallway and out through the Miphtan.

Haefen wouldn't have been asked to leave just because he failed to walk through the Qodesh wall. As far as Aron knew, Mahan was the only one who'd ever been kicked out of the community.

And what had his father been yelling about?

Aron ran toward the clearing. It was early yet, and the paths were empty for the most part. The few people he saw were surprised to see him running on the Sabbath, but no one commented. They'd assume he had a good reason. Aron wished he knew what the reason was.

47

The spiraling path went around and around as Haefen and Laurelin descended the mountain peak. Maybe they were hiking faster, but the path seemed shorter on the way down. Laurelin didn't speak, and Haefen's heart was too full.

When they emerged from the tunnel, they followed a path southward. It led them to the clearing behind the dining hall.

Brother Efrat stood in the clearing, waiting for them. He stepped forward when they approached, blocking the entrance to the dining hall. "I'm sorry for the disruption this morning, Haefen. I hope it didn't diminish your joy. I've sworn the brethren to secrecy for now, and I'd like you to take the same vow. The community isn't ready to understand what took place this morning."

"I'll gladly take a vow of silence," Haefen said, "though I must tell you I've already spoken of it to Laurelin."

A smile flickered across Brother Efrat's face. "That's of no consequence if she'll but take the same vow."

Laurelin shrugged. "I won't say anything."

Brother Efrat nodded. "Thank you. Now I'm sorry, but in order to preserve the harmony of the community, I must ask you both to leave."

"Yes," Haefen said. "I'd planned to leave in the morning, anyway."

Brother Efrat frowned. "You misunderstand me. I'm asking you to leave immediately."

Haefen gaped. "You're asking me to travel on the Sabbath? To run from the Shechinah as though I've committed a crime?"

Brother Efrat placed a hand on Haefen's shoulder. "I regret you must travel on the Sabbath, but I feel it's warranted in this case."

Laurelin snorted. "Is Brother Fredrik going to have a fit if Haefen stays here any longer? Very kingly of him."

Brother Efrat sighed. "Brother Fredrik has had a great shock. He needs time to come to terms with it."

"Why must Laurelin leave?" Haefen said. "She still needs help to return home."

They turned as Aron emerged from the dining hall carrying Haefen and Laurelin's belongings. Aron hesitated when he saw the sorrow on Haefen's face.

Haefen stepped closer and took his pack. "Thank you for bringing our things, Aron." Haefen bit his lip, and twisted the ring around his finger. "Brother Efrat said this ring once belonged to King Beraqel, so it rightly belongs to you now."

Aron shook his head. "Keep it, Haefen. The ring chose you. It should remain with you until it chooses another." Aron snorted and turned to Brother Efrat. "Can we not mention to my father how I refused the ring? I'd rather not add that to my list of failings."

Brother Efrat smiled sadly. "You're a good son, Aron. Don't let your father's criticisms make you believe otherwise."

Aron handed Laurelin her bag of belongings. "Olivia gathered them for you." He smiled. "You're still wearing the dragon pendant. I'm sorry you have to go. I wanted to get to know you better."

She smiled. "I'm sorry, too. Could you tell Olivia and Brother Udi goodbye for me?"

"Of course."

The air rippled, and Brother Sigurd appeared, the massive wooden doors open behind him. "Come with me," he said, holding out his hands to Laurelin and Haefen. His voice radiated warmth. "I have something to show you."

Brother Efrat smiled at Haefen. "It's been a pleasure to come to know you. And you as well," he said to Laurelin. "May you both arrive safely at journey's end, and may we meet again when peace has been restored."

"Thank you," Haefen said. "And thank you for your kindness and help, Brother Efrat. I'll always treasure the things I learned here."

Laurelin took one of Brother Sigurd's hands, and Haefen took the other. Haefen had been confused and anxious ever since the crystal chest cracked open at his feet. But when he took Brother Sigurd's hand, a measure of peace entered his soul.

The three of them turned, and Brother Sigurd led them through the open doorway and into the long, stone hallway beyond. The massive doors swung shut with a whisper, leaving them standing in a bright bubble of light.

Brother Sigurd's voice was warm. "You've had a rough time, Haefen, on what should have been a glorious day."

"It was glorious. To begin with, at least."

Brother Sigurd nodded. "I can see your power has grown. Follow me, and I'll find a path of peace for you to celebrate what remains of your day. I can help you as well, Laurelin McCloud. I know you yearn to return home."

Laurelin stared. "You can help me get back to the Shimmertree?"

Brother Sigurd smiled. "Not precisely."

He turned and glided down the long hallway, his cream-colored robe billowing around him.

Haefen and Laurelin followed. The smooth stone floor was more pleasant under his weary feet than the cobblestone path they'd followed to the clearing.

The bubble of brighter light moved with them as they plodded along. Haefen was weak with hunger, and tired from his interrupted sleep. He'd been wrenched from joy into a storm of tension. And now he'd been cast out of the community, away from the light of the Shechinah. He missed it already.

He bit his lip. Laurelin would return to her own planet now. Maybe one day he'd make the trek to the Shimmertree and plead with the Guardian to visit her there. He'd learn to read the symbols she'd carved into the leather flap of his pack.

When he glanced at Laurelin, she met his gaze. Haefen's heart caught in his chest. Would she miss him as much as he'd miss her? They'd only known one another a few weeks. More likely, she'd go back to her life, her family and friends, and forget about him.

Haefen counted the doors as they passed to distract himself from that thought. He'd counted nineteen doors on the left, and twenty-three doors on the right, before Brother Sigurd came to a stop.

The next door was unmarked, as all the others had been, except for a pair of white boots resting on the floor beside it. The Miphtan was too far away to be seen down the long stretch of hallway that remained.

"Brother Sigurd," Laurelin said. "What will we do about food? We haven't even had breakfast, and it's a long walk back to Phonteh. And our clothes," she said, gesturing to Haefen's white tunic and her own cream-colored dress. "We should have left them with the Puerán."

Brother Sigurd smiled. "Not to worry." He gestured with his right hand, and Haefen and Laurelin were dressed in their own clean clothing, the swamp stains laundered away by the Puerán.

Haefen had forgotten how short Laurelin's pants were. He dragged his eyes away from her bare legs. His feet were still bare. He wiggled his toes and grinned. Part of him remained in the community, an annoyance for Brother Fredrik, even if it were only his worn pair of shoes.

He could make himself a new pair of shoes from the flap on his pack, as he'd done for Laurelin. But only by destroying the gift she'd given him.

Brother Sigurd stooped and picked up the pair of white boots. "These will fit you, Haefen. Don't cut up your pack."

Haefen took the boots and turned them in his hands. He'd never seen their like. They shone with a luster more like metal than leather. But they slipped easily on his feet, and adjusted themselves to fit. Much like the ring fit his finger. "Thank you, Brother Sigurd."

"You're most welcome, Haefen. And now you must leave the sacred mountain and follow your path where it leads you. I'll fill your pack with food for your journey."

Haefen's empty pack suddenly dragged down his shoulder. Judging by the weight, he'd have plenty of food for the long hike back to Phonteh. "Thank you, Brother Sigurd. For your thoughtfulness, and your generosity."

Brother Sigurd gripped the handle of the door beside them. Sunlight streamed in through the doorway when he opened the door. He stepped aside, and Haefen caught his breath to see the Domarring's stone circle.

Laurelin gaped. "How did you do that? And how does this help me get back to the Shimmertree?"

"Not to worry," Brother Sigurd said. "This path will take you back to Earth. Travel in peace, Haefen. And you as well, Laurelin. May Abba El always guide your steps."

"Thank you for your help," Laurelin said. "For the clothes, and the food, and for this too." She gestured toward the open doorway.

Haefen stepped through first, leaving Laurelin and Brother Sigurd in the hallway behind him. But when Laurelin joined him in the midst of the stone pillars, the hallway was gone.

Laurelin spun around, gazing at the surrounding prairie. She laughed. "I guess this means I get to follow you to

Phonteh."

She sounded delighted to be stranded so far from her home. Haefen chuckled. So different from the last time they were here.

His stomach rumbled.

Laurelin grinned. "Let's eat before you pass out."

"An excellent idea."

He stepped outside the circle before settling onto the prairie grass and opening his pack. The summer sun beat down, wrapping him in warmth. "We can camp here today. Because of Brother Sigurd's kindness, we needn't travel on the Sabbath."

His pack was full of delicacies. Haefen spread the food out on the grass.

Laurelin sat beside him and took an apple and a slice of sweet bread. "Brother Sigurd gave us a feast. Is there anything to drink?"

Haefen dug in his pack. With all this food, he wouldn't even need to hunt on their homeward journey. Haefen found Laurelin's water bottle at the bottom of the pack, and fished it out. "Look what I've found." Though it had been filled with juice instead of water.

Laurelin laughed. "I forgot about my water bottle. Do you have my flip-flops too?"

Haefen found her flimsy shoes and set them beside her. "Now," he said smiling, "is there anything else or may I eat my breakfast?"

"Eat! This bread is delicious."

Haefen bit into an apple and took a handful of nuts. It was over. He'd done it.

He twisted the ring still nestling snugly on his finger. A circle in a circle. He still didn't know his father's name, but the ring proclaimed his heritage. Because of the ring, he'd been able to enter the Qodesh as he'd longed to do. He'd made covenants and received a boon of power from on high.

"Goodness," Laurelin said. "You look even happier than you did at the storytelling."

"That must be because I am." Haefen took a sip of juice from Laurelin's bottle. It tasted like nectar. He broke off a piece of cheese. "I don't understand why that happened with the crystal chest, but I know my life is acceptable to Abba El. What could make me happier than that?"

"I'm glad. Thanks for letting me tag along." She chuckled.

"What's so funny?"

"I was just thinking, we both got new shoes on this trip, but I like mine better than yours. My scabs are all gone, though." She tugged off the shoes he'd made her, and put on her old ones. "These feel strange now, it's been so long."

Haefen pulled off one of his white boots. Because they fit his feet so well, the boots were more comfortable than even his shoes had been. "They remind me of King Beraqel's breastplate, actually. The breastplate was just as white, and the material is similar."

Laurelin poked the boot. "Weird, and kinda high tech."

"High teck?"

"Like something you'd see in a special factory on my planet."

"Maybe Brother Sigurd found the boots on your world, Laurelin."

"Maybe. Or maybe on some other planet altogether."

"Interesting." Haefen stroked the boot. "They could have come from any one of Abba El's worlds."

They ate until they were full, then lay back on the grass and gazed at the blue sky. A wisp of a cloud passed overhead, blown on a summer breeze. Haefen loved the Shechinah, but he'd missed the open dome of the sky. Brother Sigurd had found him a path of peace, just as he'd said.

Laurelin stretched and sat up. "It's nice not to have to go anywhere or do anything. And thank goodness we didn't have to claw our way through the swamp again."

Haefen chuckled and sat cross-legged beside her. "That is a blessing. My family will be surprised when we return so soon. They'll think we ran all the way to Phonteh."

"I get a shock every time I see your bald head. It'll be nice when your hair grows back."

Haefen shrugged and rubbed his bare scalp. "Lucky me, I can't see it."

Their eyes met, and they smiled. A long smile that made Haefen forget to breathe.

Laurelin jumped and grabbed the pouch hanging from her neck. She pulled out the Shimmertree leaf, still as green and alive as the first time Haefen had seen it.

"Something's wrong," she said. "It's always kind of pulsed, but now it's tugging like it wants to get away. And the Guardian said not to lose it."

She stood, gripping the leaf with both hands. "What do you think it means?"

"I don't know," Haefen said. "I've never known of anyone else who had a leaf from the Tree."

Laurelin's outline started to blur.

"Laurelin!" Haefen scrambled to his feet. He stared, fighting to imprint every detail of her face in his mind. "I'll find you, Laurelin."

He reached for her, but she blurred completely, then disappeared. Haefen was alone on the prairie.

He dropped to his knees. He could still see the imprint she'd made in the prairie grass. How would he find her?

He'd probably never see her again.

Haefen picked up her water bottle and turned it in his hands, watching the juice slosh inside it. This was all he had to remember Laurelin, the girl from Earth.

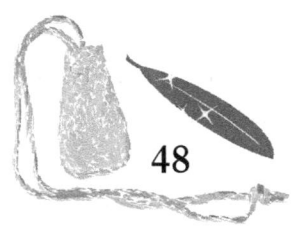

48

Haefen's words rang through her mind. "I'll find you, Laurelin." Haefen, with his crooked, heart-stopping smile. His brilliant blue eyes were the last thing she saw before he blurred and faded from sight. She didn't even have a chance to say goodbye.

Laurelin blinked and turned around. Her bag of belongings lay at her feet. A cold breeze toyed with her hair, and the Shimmertree rustled above her. She rubbed her bare arms and shivered in her shorts.

She would have known where she was just by the heady smell of the white fruit. Her mouth watered, even though she'd just eaten.

"Welcome back, Laurelin. I've been expecting you."

Piqqeah's Guardian stood beside the Tree, shimmering in his white robe. He stretched forth his hand, and the leaf flew from her grasp and up into the branches.

"But that leaf came from Earth's Shimmertree, not Piqqeah's."

"The Trees are one, Laurelin."

Everything was happening quickly now, after her peaceful week on Mount Nevo. But her dad would be going crazy, and she missed him. And she couldn't wait to see Benjamin with his sticky fingers and jam-smeared face. It was time to go home.

The Guardian brought a branch within reach, and pointed. "Pluck this leaf."

The cluster of fruit nestling beside the leaf smelled so

enticing, that almost without thinking, she tried to pick one. Her hand went right through it, of course.

"Sorry." Laurelin grasped the Shimmertree leaf with her right hand. It pulsed between her fingers, familiar, yet still so strange. She gazed one last time at the snowy mountains surrounding the Shimmertree valley, and plucked the leaf off the branch.

"Welcome back, Laurelin. I've been expecting you."

Earth's Guardian stretched his hand toward Laurelin, and the leaf flew up to join the others.

"Why don't the leaves die after I've picked them from the Tree?"

"Because you're never out of range of Ben El's love and power, no matter where you travel within Abba El's dominion. He gave the Tree life, and he extends that life to any portion of the Tree, wherever it may be."

Laurelin took a deep breath, filling her lungs with the exhilarating scent of the fruit. "My family must think I'm dead, I've been gone so long. And all I wanted was to taste the fruit. Do you promise I'll be able to eat one someday?"

The Guardian smiled. "That's up to you. Now, you can't take Jeffree's book back to Pleasant Knoll."

Laurelin crouched and opened the bag. She put on her watch, then flipped through the book. She couldn't read the words any more. She shrugged, and handed it to the Guardian.

"I'll give you a book to replace it," he said. He reached into the air, took a book from somewhere else, and handed it to Laurelin.

The new book had a hard blue cover. It said "Journal" on the front, and had a Supermart price tag stuck to the back. She snorted. "You took this from my dad's store?"

"It seemed appropriate. His store has been reimbursed. Record the experiences you had on Piqqeah, Laurelin, lest you forget."

Forget? How could she ever forget Haefen? "Sure, if

you want me to. Can I go back to Piqqeah someday?"

"That's not my decision to make. Travel in peace, Laurelin."

"Thanks. You too."

The Guardian, shimmering in his white robe, stepped behind the Tree and was gone.

At least he hadn't said no.

Laurelin took another deep breath, savoring the scent of the fruit, then started down the grassy slope of the endless Shimmertree hill. She had a long hike ahead of her. But after a few steps, the hill compressed until it was the low, green hill she'd first seen all those days ago. She jogged the rest of the way down and across the canyon floor.

Laurelin stopped short after she'd pushed through the hanging roots and stepped through the archway. She'd forgotten she had no way to get home.

She could walk to Pleasant Knoll, or she could hitchhike. Strolling along the edge of the highway wasn't a great idea. But some axe murderer would probably pick her up if she stuck out her thumb.

She hadn't missed home all that much on Piqqeah. But now that she was back on Earth, her heart ached to get back to her family. All she wanted was to give Benjamin a hug.

Maybe there'd be a pay phone in the park. Did they still make pay phones? If her dad hadn't taken her cell phone she could have called for help.

She felt the familiar anger gather in her chest. But Laurelin shook her head and let it go. Her father wouldn't have taken her phone if she hadn't broken the rules. And her phone would have been dead by now, anyway.

She hurried along the base of the ridge, around the oak tree, then over and around the rocks. Then she turned her back on the ridge and walked straight west.

She was a bit off and never saw the boulder where she'd eaten her turkey sandwich. But she found the path she'd taken.

She jogged along it through the trees and back toward the park.

Laurelin heard voices.

They couldn't still be searching for her, not after two weeks. But some other group might have come to the park. She could borrow a phone and call her dad. He'd probably freak when he heard her voice. Maybe Benjamin would answer.

She was breathless when the path ended at the field of parched grass. A youth group had scattered around playing badminton and croquet. Some of the kids were eating lunch.

Laurelin stared. She recognized them.

"Did you have a nice walk, honey?"

Laurelin whirled to see a woman standing by the picnic table. She gestured toward an assortment of half-empty chip bags and a few squashed sandwiches. "Still hungry? I was worried when you went off by yourself. I'm glad you weren't gone any longer."

"What do you mean? How long was I gone?"

"Oh, forty minutes, maybe."

Laurelin stopped gaping and forced herself to smile. "Right."

"Want some chips?"

"Uh. No, thank you."

Laurelin wandered over and sat on the prickly grass to watch the kids play badminton. Her fingers strayed to the sea-tooth dragon hanging beside her empty pouch. She grinned.

All that worry for nothing. Her dad never even knew she was gone.

Laurelin watched the shuttlecock fly back and forth across the net.

She'd come back here on her own and visit the Shimmertree. Even if the Guardian didn't let her go anywhere, she'd get to smell the fruit again.

She rubbed the Supermart sticker on the journal he'd

given her. No, first she'd write all about Piqqeah and Haefen. Then the Guardian would be more likely to let her go back.

She smiled. Pleasant Knoll wasn't such a bad place to live after all.

49

The breeze caressed Haefen's face, bringing him the scent of the sea. He was almost home.

He'd left the Domarring early that morning, even before the sun had risen above the horizon. It had set long since. But he hungered to be home, and his new boots ate up the distance.

His thoughts had wandered during his long day. He'd fingered the auger where it hung under his shirt and thought about what he'd learned in the Qodesh. He thought about the Puerán. He twirled the ring around his finger.

He had relived the moment the crystal chest opened, and remembered Brother Fredrik's stricken face when his hands passed through the armor. How vexing for him, to see his dream in ashes. Haefen felt only compassion for him.

But most of the time, his thoughts had wandered toward Laurelin. Haefen would have given up if she hadn't been there to support him. She'd cheered him on when he'd lost all hope of entering the Qodesh. Because of her, he'd been willing to try harder. To work until he was exhausted. To fight past his failures until he prevailed.

Rohbert would need his help on the farm these next few months. But after that, Haefen would make the long trek to the Shimmertree. He'd ask the Guardian how to find Laurelin so he could tell her thank you. She'd believed in him when he'd had no one else. And he missed her smile already.

And while Haefen was at the Tree, he'd ask the

Guardian a few more questions. Like, who left the king's ring under the Domarring altar stone? Why had the ring chosen him? Why had the crystal chest opened for him, instead of Brother Fredrik?

And most important of all the questions teeming through Haefen's soul, what was his father's name? And what kind of man had he been?

The stars watched over Haefen, guiding him westward along the Jylboa River toward Phonteh. He passed old Jaron's hut, and his pace quickened. Just a bit farther.

And then he was there. Haefen eased open the door.

His parents were still up, chatting by the fire. Rute dropped her mending and sprang to her feet, catching Haefen in a big hug. "You're back! We never expected you so soon."

Rohbert grabbed Haefen next, and hugged him tight. "We missed you, son." He stepped back and chuckled, stroking Haefen's bare scalp. "You did it! But why are you back so soon? Is everything all right?"

Haefen grinned. "Everything is wonderful. And I'm so glad to be home."

END OF BOOK 1

This story continues in Shimmertree Chronicles Book 2, when Haefen and Laurelin fight off the Sons of Darkness to find the sword of King Beraqel. Pre-register at shimmertree.com to be notified when Book 2 is available in 2015.

Also by Robyn Oakes:
In **Two Trees**, see the city of Betavar transformed into Asseldam by the Sons of Darkness. An epic quest, a magical adventure, a knife fight with an evil sorcerer, and finding a love any girl would fight dragons for.

Annor, 16 years old, is living isolated and alone. The Guardian gives her a choice: He can send her back to live a normal life in the city of her parents. Or she can follow the harder path her father intended for her. If she follows that path, she'll find more joy than she could imagine. But on the way, she'll pass through fear into terror. Alone.
Two paths. Two trees. Which should she choose?

See everywhere Robyn Oakes' books are sold at shimmertree.com

ABOUT THE AUTHOR

Robyn was born in the Rocky Mountains, but grew up in southern California. She received the top academic scholarship from Brigham Young University and attended BYU before serving an 18-month mission in Sweden for the Church of Jesus Christ of Latter-day Saints.

After her mission, Robyn graduated magna cum laude from San Diego State University with a bachelor's degree in English and a minor in Business. She married shortly thereafter and gave birth to two sons and a daughter before returning to SDSU and earning a master's degree in English in 1996. She currently lives with her husband in Riverton, Utah.

Robyn has wanted to be a writer since second grade. She dreamed up the Shimmertree while writing her master's thesis comparing the world creations of Narnia, Middle-earth, and Genesis.

www.ingramcontent.com/pod-product-compliance
Lightning Source LLC
Chambersburg PA
CBHW060922180626
46817CB00004B/1360